BS

Christine Jordis

RAPTURE

Translated from the French by
Sonia Soto

Harvill
Secker

First published with the title *La chambre blanche* by Editions du Seuil, 2003

2 4 6 8 10 9 7 5 3 1

Copyright © Editions du Seuil, 2003
English translation copyright © Sonia Soto, 2005

First published in Great Britain in 2005 by Harvill/Secker
Random House, 20 Vauxhall Bridge Road,
London SW1V 2SA

Random House Australia (Pty) Limited,
20 Alfred Street, Milsons Point,
Sydney, New South Wales 2061, Australia

Random House New Zealand Limited
18 Poland Road, Glenfield, Auckland 10, New Zealand

Random House South Africa (Pty) Limited
Endulini, 5A Jubilee Road, Parktown 2193, South Africa

The Random House Group Limited Reg. No. 954009
www.randomhouse.co.uk

Ouvrage traduit avec le concours du Ministère Français chargé de la Culture –
Centre National du Livre

This book is published with support from the French Ministry of Culture –
Centre National du Livre

This book is supported by the French Ministry of Foreign Affairs, as part of
the Burgess Programme headed for the French Embassy in London by the
Institut Français du Royaume-Uni

A CIP catalogue record for this book
is available from the British Library

ISBN 1 84343 102 5

Typeset in Monotype Fournier by
Palimpsest Book Production Ltd, Polmont, Stirlingshire

Printed and bound in Great Britain by William Clowes Ltd, Beccles, Suffolk

'My purpose is to see in eroticism an aspect of man's inner life, of his religious life, if you like.' Georges Bataille, *Eroticism*

'What is frightening is the loss of the sacred in the human, particularly in sexual relations, because it means that no true union is possible.'
Marguerite Yourcenar, in an interview with Shusha Guppy

A friend

I learned of Camille's death one evening in September 1992. By chance, in a conversation with old friends from university. We were in the habit of meeting once a year, to exchange news, smooth the passage of time, resume an enduring conversation that, over the years, beyond the events that separated us, created a form of reassuring continuity in our lives. That evening someone mentioned Camille's death. A car accident, on her way back from Italy, where she'd lived for years, alone and happy to be so, in a small rented house in a village.

This news made me recall her face, the slight, mysterious smile when she preferred to say nothing rather than answer, her slow steady way of speaking, my surprise when one day she handed me a manuscript and said: 'So that you should know me better.' It was one of the last times I saw her.

A strange woman, Camille, rather inscrutable, her enigmatic quality, in my view, constituting her essential charm. They say you shouldn't judge by appearances: even less so in her case than in others.

I met her through a mutual friend at the beginning of the 1980s. She was no longer young, she must have been over fifty, and yet, more than her words or her story, which was rather banal when I thought about it, her looks were what first struck me. Not that there was, at first sight, anything remarkable about her, though she was still pretty, in a discreet way – brown hair and grey-green eyes – but it was her gaze that held your attention. It was thoughtful and intense. In the literary circles in which I move, people would generally rather be heard than listen, rather be seen than see – or see out of simple curiosity, not a desire to understand. Such a gaze, therefore, which rested upon you calmly and took the whole of you in, assuring you of a presence, was not common. I wanted to get to know better the one who possessed it.

She told me that she had lived in the country for some years, alone with an elderly mother. She was teaching then, seventeenth- and eighteenth-century French literature, I think. When her mother died, she moved to Paris and got a job at the Ministry of Culture – one of those safe jobs that leave you enough peace of mind to lead your life – and gave up teaching. From her solitary, somewhat stifling existence, she retained a reserve – like a distance that came between her and the person she was talking to which gave her time to reflect during a conversation. I saw this barely perceptible withdrawal as a distinctive trait, the sign of a mind that searched, took its time, went into things in depth, more concerned to express a truth than to produce an effect.

In public you didn't notice her, she had no particular sparkle or vitality.

Camille had the extensive culture of people who have spent their childhood in relative isolation, without many outside resources or the distraction of television (it still wasn't very common in those days), alone with their books and in them seeking the adventure and excitement lacking in their daily lives. The strong emotions she craved, she found in the Romantics and the mystics. She often spoke to me of these friends. In adolescence, such books move you, but some people remain attached to them their entire lives – those who like to recall their rebellious and demanding younger selves, or who maintain over the years an attitude thought to be specific to youth. As if middle and old age were nothing but a long succession of acts of cowardice and compromise. A process of adapting to everything until your interior contours are lost.

And she wrote, notes, fragments, a diary, and this manuscript, which she had not tried to publish but gave me to read as a sign of confidence. Her style was visibly inspired by her reading, influenced by her Catholic upbringing, shaped by sex, death and guilt. And yet I was moved by the intensity of the feelings she described – envious no doubt.

After all, more often than not we live with a sort of general boredom, busy, if not frantically overworked, but only on the surface, distracted by information, which is only an approximate form of culture, anaesthetised rather than stimulated by the news of disasters that swamps us every day, so that we feel few things deeply unless we are directly involved of course, and even then the feelings are diluted, quickly covered over. Lives dominated by the desire above all that nothing should happen, by the feeling that only unfortunate things occur and that tranquillity is the highest good we can hope for. The boredom I felt was that of an entire society whose last resort was irony, permanent derision, relying on carefully cultivated detachment, this detachment – or should one say disenchantment? – also linked to a sort of powerlessness. Furthermore, the few experiences we're sufficiently favoured to have are determined by fashions and a vocabulary that, far from opening the field to our potential, tend, whatever one thinks, to restrict rather than expand it. Thus, the thought systems that surround the contemporary lover like a wall leave no room for love – or they devalue it. And the language at its disposal buries it, oppresses it, pushes it aside.

The affair whose highs and lows Camille wrote of with such candour made me feel sorry I had never known anything similar. True, I am younger than her, and my childhood was spent in a freer, easier world, but at these moments when I think of her again I do wonder what my life amounts to. My 'career', as they say? The routine of daily tasks, coming and going at set times, a structure in a way imposed from outside: my job relieves me of concern for myself, which is important, I admit. I can almost fill my days while being absent from myself, 'functioning' as a well-oiled, high-performance machine, or at least so I hope in my hours of optimism. And all these 'things to do' that impose a rhythm upon time, drive the feeling of emptiness from it, ease the anxiety. Days filled to bursting point, a timetable expertly organised so as to distract from the hollowness, the feeling of floating that would allow questioning to arise. 'What is it all for?' Such is after all the fate of people who are lucky enough to work, and I'm not complaining. On the contrary, I'm aware how fortunate I am, while sometimes asking myself, knowing full well that I have no answer, whether I am alive, yes, whether I'm really living. Others no doubt ask themselves the same question, people who, like me, play all their different roles as best they can – civil servants, soldiers, doctors and lawyers, bosses or employees, fathers and mothers, husbands and wives, in our private and in our social lives, since we're permanently acting on both fronts, like brave little soldiers.

That's why Camille's book moved me, since it was a possible answer to this persistent question that we try to push aside, more often than not successfully.

To rediscover her one last time, to revive her memory before it disappeared, I decided to return to the copy of the manuscript that she gave me. This is what I read:

1

Boredom, sometimes called availability

Throughout the next day, after our first embrace, I spoke to him in my mind, recounting, commenting on our conversations of the day before, narrating the various episodes of my day as I lived them. Towards evening, I became lost in myself and his memory became unreal. I could no longer find or even imagine him. All that remained was a vague, guilty desire.

Thus, after the intense mental activity of the past few hours – an activity which undoubtedly lacked variety since it was focused entirely on a single object – I returned to that white space without form or contours, without contrasts or rough edges, without major annoyances or intense excitement, which was my usual state, in other words before I met Julien.

Not that anything specific was missing. Being alone did not bother me, I had friends, not many, but enough, my work occupied me and, though not thrilling, I enjoyed it. I mixed with a circle of more or less literary people, which suited my tastes. I had just turned forty and, while I felt old some days, I felt it less frequently, however, than when I was twenty. No, there seemed to be nothing missing, and yet the essential (but what was the essential?) was lacking from my life.

Day after day life went by, unchanging despite numerous tiny variations, without my feeling truly involved in it. But in the impossibility of reaching – what? I didn't know – I had ended up finding an identity of sorts.

A state of semi-paralysis devoid, to my mind, of any interest. Yet I could not help noticing that, at the time, it was the inspiration for a fair number of the books whose reading I was meant to promote. How many books had as their subject the writer's torment before a blank page reflecting back at him his own emptiness, unless – but the effect was the same – it was the virgin page that created within him a void that he overcame, most of the time, only through laborious and rather artificial exercises. In their abundance, the books about this existential problem ended up constituting an easily recognisable genre. To my unhappiness, therefore, was added not only the certainty that this was a commonplace phenomenon, but the rather grim prospect of seeing my own efforts rewarded by a result that I already deemed very modest, judging by the examples on offer at least.

This secret malaise had not, however, prevented me from achieving a certain authority in my professional life: in the office at the Ministry of Culture where I held a modest position, people listened to my opinions. Moreover, as I have said, it gave me a kind of security, simply because it had lasted so long: the security that comes from the certainty of moving on familiar ground. I had acquired, in the presence of others, not assurance, indeed, I wouldn't go that far, but — something that I appreciated no less — the gift of invisibility. I had earned sufficient autonomy to look, to look endlessly, without expecting to be seen. And I gloried in a peace that I knew deep down was, nevertheless, simply a kind of death.

Then, one day, the splendid equilibrium that for years I had done my best to maintain was shattered. Of course it wasn't as sudden as such a statement might lead one to believe. At first, despite my huge desire for change, I experienced only fear and a feeling of refusal when it occurred.

The fact is, I was not in the least prepared for what was going to happen. Love was not an event I was expecting. I had deeply rooted fears and prejudices, reservations that covered secret desire like a slab of concrete, to which was added a propensity for criticism and irony — a tendency which denotes a certain desiccation of one's being or, at the very least, a defence system sufficiently practised to protect one from flights of emotion. Without, as the Ancients did, locating the seat of love-induced disorder in the liver or the brain, or calling it melancholy — the term used by Robert Burton in *The Anatomy of Melancholy*, a book that I had enjoyed — I almost considered love a sickness accompanied by fever and obsessive symptoms, a fixation of the mind on a single being, depriving one of the freedom to be interested in the rest of the world or to live at peace with oneself, a violent crisis followed by a more or less long and always painful convalescence, and of which one day at last nothing remained . . .

Until then I had relied on my own resources – in other words on friendship, encounters, travel, and career changes, in which I invariably took the initiative – to cause the superficial renewals without which one stops being aware of life. These were, of course, nothing but superficial changes. As for moments of real life – those moments when external things become internal and seem to pulse within us – only rarely was I granted one. If all my life I had been concerned with finding a way to prolong them (the periods of real life), trying to ensure that they constituted the fabric of my days and not isolated instances, separate from the others with which they had no link, I had never found the way. As far as I could judge, their emergence was connected neither to circumstances nor to my efforts. And it did not seem that love was the way to induce or multiply them.

In the very early days of our meetings, surprised that I recoiled at the prospect of an experience that most people would welcome or even seek out, Julien asked me: 'So without it, without the possibility of falling in love, how do you manage to renew yourself?' I answered a little pompously (I was starting to lose my instinct for irony), evoking the malaise which meant that one was never at ease in life and that, perpetually seeking adjustment, one avoided the risk, that had seemed so frightening when I was younger, of sinking into a tranquillity consisting of routine and death. Thus I had long feared as a threat the bliss displayed by those busy nesting mothers, whose only claim to glory was having satisfied the laws of instinct and who, with their placid contentment, had always caused me anxiety and slight revulsion. But suffering that stretches on and becomes a habit is no longer stimulating, it soon turns into another form of comfort. Also, as I was formulating my answer, I was aware of how inadequate it was.

An ideal moment

In life, true encounters are a question of moment, of a coincidence in timing, as much as of affinity, we have all noticed it. Availability is one of the essential conditions for love, as some great minds have pointed out. Thus, Roland Barthes: 'The subject is in a sense empty, available, offered unwittingly to the rape which will surprise him*.'

Day after day, we rush from one task to another, from one goal to the next, like trains stopping at fixed times at station after station whose route never varies (the life of young Werther, before he meets Charlotte, has also been described as 'a blank and prosaic daily round, lulling him'). The regular rhythm of the lulling sends one to sleep, as does habit, this is one of the risks of busy ordered lives. They lack the essential, which is momentum.

One might imagine a moment in life located between innocence (in other words absolute ignorance of oneself and the other) and experience (which often corresponds to lassitude: anything but to fall in love again and be as miserable once

---

*This quotation is taken from *A Lover's Discourse – Fragments*, translated by Richard Howard, Farrar, Straus and Giroux 1978, as are all the Barthes quotations included in this book.

more), an ideal moment therefore, in which the mature indi-
vidual, still having lived little (or not enough, depending on
his view) and tired of a long internal drought, has without
knowing it prepared himself for love and is waiting for it with
all his being. It is in this period of one's life, at a distance
from both blind groping and exhaustion, that they say great
loves are lived.

2

The meeting

We met at a public lecture, in Paris one evening. I cannot even say, as in those romantic novels where it all begins with love at first sight, that this first meeting made a strong impression on me: in fact I barely noticed Julien among his group of friends.

A few days later, however, having found out my name and address, he called, to see me again, speak to me, ask me out for a drink, or a meal, whatever you like, he said. Was it audacity on his part, as he later maintained with a kind of surprise, or simply one of the many ploys that enabled him constantly to approach new people, soon learning to get to know them and seduce them, so that his life, far from sinking into habit, benefited from constant change, from an ever-renewed measure of excitement? I was intrigued, and sufficiently curious and available to accept. If I look at the years and months preceding this invitation, I see that I was waiting, for that or another, with all my being, even if I did not yet know it.

From that very first telephone conversation, I was struck by his voice, quick and hesitant, modulated, insistent, its caress conveying all the nuances of his feelings.

A voice that was alive. Later on when, after weeks of silence, I heard him on the telephone, his tone seemed to resonate directly within me, as if my whole body were receiving it. By its familiar music alone, without my even trying to grasp the sense, each sentence overwhelmed me.

And yet, the first time I saw Julien, I can't remember feeling any emotions other than expectation and curiosity. Nothing in his appearance was surprising, nothing, at first sight, predicted the combination of gentleness and concern, the unbridled desire to please that constituted the core of his nature and which, later on, seemed to me to emanate from every expression and attitude, from the slightest gesture; a sensibility always on the alert, refined in the extreme, that was served by his evident sensuality. But I was undoubtedly more concerned with analysing the effect he had on me than on reading the expressions that succeeded one another upon his mobile face.

This calm interest was nothing like the excitement that had gripped me one day when, lying on a bank of the River Cam, in Cambridge, during a holiday in my distant student days, I had seen the figure of a young man to whom I was immediately attracted, heading in my direction, standing at the back of one of those flat boats called punts. Just as I was making a wish to meet him, a wish I thought would never come true given my extreme shyness, this prince charming, as if drawn magnetically by my desire, approached me and, sitting down beside me, began to talk to me.

Several times, I had experienced, not 'love at first sight', since the love implied by that expression was lacking, but a desire that, like electricity flowing between two poles, from the very first look touches two beings simultaneously: love at first sense.

Perhaps it was the insignificance of his appearance that reassured me in the beginning; indeed, what need did I have for beauty or easy seduction, for a display of self-confidence, I, who lived, after years of abstinence, in caution born of fear and whom too evident an intention, too obvious a savoir-faire would only have deterred, emphasising my feeling of difference? In fact, Julien had the savoir-faire that his slightly indecisive manner seemed to preclude, to the point of genius, for his skill was not based on any vulgar 'trick', any acquired knowledge; actually, it depended little on experience, but rather on an intuitive gift, a sensitivity towards the other that was almost prophetic. What's more, his discreet, unremarkable appearance, suited my sense of secrecy; it contributed to my impression of discovering little by little that which was hidden: a charm that seemed to fit needs that I did not suspect, my most intimate desires, when in fact it fitted many other needs than mine, many other desires.

*

As I have said, nothing about him struck me as remarkable the first time; I was too busy examining my own impressions, all my critical faculties alerted by a combination of ease and shyness, hesitancy and assurance that I could not unravel. Is it an instinct of self-preservation that sharpens one's lucidity to the point at which it becomes destructive and makes one reject or question certain behaviour from the outset? From the very first hours we spent together, I suspected him of readily seeking an effect, using sentences whose power he had already tested on similar occasions, rather than pronouncing words that he had discovered or reinvented in the difficulty or spontaneity of each unique moment. But these effects were introduced so delicately and so naturally that one had to put them down to a lucky stroke of inspiration with which he was justifiably pleased, rather than to a recognised seduction technique. I mean that they would soon touch me, not because he had invented them for me, but because they testified to his talent. It's wrong to say that love is blind: on the contrary, it chooses to see and pick out the positive aspect that escaped us at first; and in that regard it is more perceptive than the state of indifference or mistrust that preceded it. How taken aback and disappointed I was sometimes when, leaving the intimacy of the flat where we met, I caught sight of Julien from a distance, in the street, lost amongst anonymous figures and so unlike my memory of him. I saw him suddenly reduced to himself, deprived of the magic with which my love surrounded him, a sad, tired little man, already marked by age. For a few intolerable minutes he was a stranger beside me. I had then to fight against myself in order to connect with him again, to find once more beneath that ordinary exterior the unique being that I had stopped perceiving for a moment. In the early days, these eclipses of my love were frequent, these moves from a world transformed by the light a person has bestowed upon it to a world deprived of that light – a dead world; and every time, a feeling of emptiness, powerlessness and anguish. But perhaps he was occupied with other thoughts when I spotted him in the crowd: he hadn't had the opportunity to concentrate, to gather himself at the prospect of our meeting, so that his face was not lit up with pleasure and, instead of the expected excitement, all I saw, for one dreadful moment, was emptiness and absence betraying his inner weariness and his distance from me.

Features that I found weak and irregular on that first occasion, I later examined one by one, tirelessly, with fascination, seeking to understand how they could move me to such an extent, always surprised that the contours whose slightest inflection I knew by heart were enough to fulfil me and that all the questions in the world could find an answer and an end in their simple assembly. The fact is, my images and memories of him had gradually been superimposed upon those features; intense, exhilarating or painful, they charged his image with meaning. Like the lines of a book in which one seeks passionately to decode the hidden meaning, they allowed traces of an existence to show through, to which my expectation, my constant straining towards him lent an inexhaustible mystery and charm. In that which I had at first disliked – the too-high forehead, made even higher by his receding hair – I now saw like a sign of his constantly active mind, contradicted and offset by the fleshy mass of his lips. I also liked what Julien most disliked, the bulging flesh around his chin, betraying his ageing and in which I saw gentleness for that very reason, because his will to seduce, which I read in his eyes and demeanour, was combined with a sign of weakness and fatigue – the passing of time, the effects of life on his face. I thus found, combined in Julien's features, two antagonistic tendencies which I was to discover could so successfully reinforce each other.

The sensuality of his mouth, which one did not notice immediately because of the expressiveness of his face – this was where I felt he was revealed best: in a fullness marked, though, by a certain disenchantment, as if, like his eyes but perhaps more so, it had the power to express a longing to live that was never quite satisfied. His mouth revealed the tensions, the desires, the anxiety inside Julien and his weariness, but also tenderness and pleasure – a fluctuating, disordered life, that eluded any attempt at appropriation and whose power to attract he was well aware of. 'However disappointed, however crushed a woman is by a failure,' he said one day, 'she has only to meet some-one a little alive and she'll love again.'

To be 'a little alive'. To me, he was life itself in a world where most people were already half-dead, trapped in narrow repetitive circuits, external routine or their own obsessions, their inability to live or change. That this vitality was linked to his wish to seduce was an obvious fact that I had to accept and for which I loved him; I could not help but feel astonished admiration at his insatiable need for novelty – I, who so rarely fell in love – at the tireless activity of desire and his ability to fall for ever different women.

Julien was then entirely occupied with my conquest, alive to the birth of a happiness that he sensed and whose arrival, as a great artist, he skilfully arranged; I was still reluctant, more concerned with analysing and understanding what was happening to me than with giving myself up to the novelty. It was only later, much later, that, subduing, as he did, the painful need to pin down that which by its very nature constantly changes and disappears, I managed to live in the moment and no longer wonder about what was to follow.

The image of my desire

'It is not every day, it has been cleverly noticed, that one meets that which is made to give one exactly the image of our desire*'. Indeed. A sentence which I would place beside this observation of Roland Barthes': 'In the encounter . . . I am like a gambler whose luck cannot fail, so that his hand unfailingly lands on the little piece which immediately completes the puzzle of his desire.'

This gradual discovery of affinities as well as of parts of a body, 'little pieces' that fit as if by a miracle a desire of which I had until then been quite unaware – no, one does not get to make such a discovery every day. There are even some lives in which such an encounter never happens, once maybe, if one is lucky. But this one time is enough to make us understand that nothing else matters, neither the days that have gone before, nor those to come.

*Lacan (*The Seminary*, 1, 163) quoted by R. Barthes in *A Lover's Discourse – Fragments*, op.cit.

3

'The ravishment'

Our second encounter was more significant perhaps.
Julien, whose work as an art historian caused him to spend
a great deal of time in museums, invited me to visit an
exhibition of sculptures by Camille Claudel, in local
gardens that at the time had an out-of-the-way, countri-
fied feel, which they have since lost due to the influx of
tourists. One of these sculptures, called 'The Waltz', held
our attention longer than the others. It was of a man and
a woman, whirling, their arms around each other, leaning
with the intensity of their movement. The woman's body,
bent by her partner's embrace, is given up entirely to the
momentum that sweeps her along; her head is resting
against the man's; the dress slipping from her shoulders,
unfurls and swirls at her feet; so that the mingled bodies
seem to form a single long oblique line, one end constituted by the two overlapping heads, the other by the
seething cloth, that resembles foaming water. The irresistible movement of the dance, the momentum of the
couple given up to it – I understood that he was giving
them to me, that the promise of life the sculpture expressed
was addressed to me. Just as Julien had intended in taking

21

me to the gardens, 'The Waltz', which conveyed to me without need of words his emotion and his pleasure, was affixed as it were like a seal – in my partiality, I readily imagined that like the heraldic arms of noble families it represented to Julien a sign of ownership and a template – at the top of the still-blank page of our story. So as to make me share in his sense of joy, he often resorted to some work of art which he contemplated at length, knowing that together his admiration and the influence of the work acted upon me, transporting me to a more elevated world, which is not the one we live in, but as Proust said, the world of which certain moments of grace give us an intuition. So I came to confuse the feeling he inspired in me with the effect produced by the art, his presence beside me with the wonder he was giving me to see. But such confusion simply testified to his power, for if I found the object he was showing me beautiful, if my perceptions had recently sharpened until they reached this degree of intensity, it was to him that I owed this, not to the harmony of the work in question, it was he who had transformed the landscape around me, endowing it with a magical vibration that made it perceptible to me at every moment.

From the very beginning, he literally tore me from myself, not letting a day pass without sending a sign to remind me of his presence the day before, weaving around me the fabric of another life, far removed from my usual world. They were heavily lined envelopes sometimes containing only a few words, a postcard, a volume of poems, a picture of a beloved object, such as the ancient vase whose black pattern stood out against a white background, with its sober solid balance, strong to the point of imposing itself like an obvious fact, and whose beauty he hoped would exert its influence on me like an ambassador, and communicate his own sense of the beauty of the world. Those few words, laid out, depending on the day or his mood, in the middle of the page or, modestly, in a corner, written in small letters or on the contrary in capitals, surprised and charmed me; even my name alone, written in ink in the full, uneven hand the mere sight of which would soon set my heart beating, preventing me at first from opening the envelope, assured me that he was thinking of me, that I was in some way chosen, since an unprecedented thing was happening: the sudden, unexpected advent, so surprising in my life, of a revival. And then the words, confirming what the sight of my name had already told me – a tremor passed through them, a hope which, even today, when I open those old letters, transmits a little of the promise they contained at that season's beginning, the coming of spring which was, he wrote, intended for me.

4

'I want to understand'

Little by little, the very texture of life changed. It was I,
I remember, who quite naturally made the first moves, just
as Julien was the first to start using the less formal *'tu'*
when we spoke to each other. People say 'to be taken with
someone', 'I'm very taken with you' he later declared,
delighted; was it the word 'taken' that amused him – you're
taken with someone just as you are taken aback or taken
by surprise – and had he waited till then to feel in turn
seduced and captivated, dominated, led? But rather than
this apparent reversal of roles perhaps it was a manifest
sign of my desires and inner impulses that he was seeking.
'It's lucky,' he said one day, 'that you know what you want
in love.' In fact, he made me discover possibilities of which
until then I had had no inkling. For if I knew what pleasure was, if I knew the violence of a spasm where the whole
world disappears, and the feeling of peace that follows,
nothing had prepared me for the depths that I would now
experience.

And yet, it was not easy losing sight of my usual landscape. Soon, considering it from a new angle, I would never
quite want to return to it, but, at that time, just before

leaving, I discovered its appeal and its advantages and I lingered there, seeking to retain some familiar fragment that would serve as a token, as proof of my old life and my identity during the strange crossing upon which I was about to embark.

A day without seeing him sometimes enabled me to return to myself, that is, to seek to understand what was happening to me. The need to understand had always mattered to me intensely; reduced to themselves, both sensation and feeling seemed inadequate and, whether suffering or joy, I could never experience anything new without immediately trying to analyse it, so as to grasp the nature and origin of an impression which I had to connect to a set of perceptions and known things. Thus, no experience was limited to itself, but opened out on to wider vistas, according to a system of similarities and echoes. Having found it a place and a meaning, I felt it belonged to me more; it assumed an interest that far exceeded its initial reach, so that my pleasure was enhanced.

5

'The good mood of desire'

Until then I had had the same liking for subtlety in my love life as I had in my habit of introspection, preferring the approach to the goal itself, desire to its fulfilment, and the movement held back for a moment to the movement completed too soon that led to sensations that were always alike because the imagination had not had a chance to prepare, build, nuance them. I found in the prolonged wait for what remains to come, in the semi-uncertainty of the other's reactions, in the entire period where curbed desire gradually becomes exasperated, conferring extreme tension upon the slightest movement, I found in the wait for love a pleasure often more exhilarating than the love itself. But I had come to do without these subtle pleasures, based at times on nothing but a glance, an allusion, a light touch that I might have imagined: the switch from a wait that has stretched on too long to the acceptance of absence is easy, and vague desire sustained over the days by arabesques in a void is just as happy to remain dimmed until such time as a true call comes seeking it out. A reminder that all this time desire has merely been asleep, impervious but ready.

So it was not without fear that one day at last I followed

Julien to the end of a quiet narrow street, to the place where he withdrew in order to work, undisturbed by any echo of daily life, any revealing trace of other activity, since he did not live there. That this place, which would from then on be the setting for our meetings, was thus separate from the realm of ordinary things, entirely devoted to thought and to love, suited my need to isolate the essential, to surround it with secrecy and contemplation. In the greater part of our lives, we play a series of parts with which we more or less identify, whether it be that of friend, observer or adviser, parent, brother or husband, but in none of these parts are we entirely ourselves, in none of them do we connect with ourselves, since they only represent a limited aspect of our personality and it may be only in the concentration of work, as in the business of love, that we overcome our inner divisions.

For the first time, though without even noticing, in the sort of waking dream that became my usual state in Julien's presence, removing me from ordinary life, so intense was it on that day in particular, I pushed open the heavy door that, like the street itself and the surrounding district, was to mark the boundary of the enchanted area where I would meet him.

Soon, going down into the entrance of my local métro station, I had only to find myself on the line where the name of his station appeared to feel with the speeding of my heart, with the change of rhythm that affected my entire being, that the descent underground, as in an initiation, preceded my entry into another world. That this world was a geographical as well as a psychological place, a district of Paris rather similar to my own, was not in the least disconcerting, since I had to travel underground to reach it, through a labyrinth of tunnels, and there was thus no continuity between it and the ordinary everyday universe. I went through the subsequent stages, the turning at the métro exit which, from a busy square led suddenly into a narrow street, the hill lined with large old houses guarded by thick dark doors, in a second state, so absorbed by the thought of being with him again that I could see nothing, hear nothing, having already withdrawn from external life which was going on around me and without me. Once inside the building, everything was dark and quiet; thick carpet muffled the sound of my footsteps, and the doors on the landings, which I never saw open, remained closed over their secret. How many hidden rendezvous like ours, how many clandestine loves and unknown meetings were taking place within these walls, in the intimacy of closed rooms? I liked to imagine that the whole place was dedicated to love, not like those nineteenth-century hotels used by prostitutes, though this well-to-do house reminded me of them, but rather like a temple where a mystery was being celebrated in which I was privileged to participate. If love, in my view, had to be surrounded by darkness and secrecy, it was to separate it from ordinary life, with which there was no comparison, rather than to promote a sense of inwardness and to increase pleasure. But this frame of mind, in a way 'religious', came upon me only gradually; my attitude was quite different the first time I stepped through the door to that place.

6

'I saw everything about his body, coldly'

At the top of the stairs, in a room that jutted out into empty space like the prow of a ship, I remember that – with more resolve than desire that time – without saying a word or waiting for his initiative, I undressed in front of him; he had not given a single sign to request this divesting that revealed me to him; I was thus signalling that the era of beginnings was at an end, even if the decision was not accompanied by any particular pleasure. I wanted Julien to see me, to take possession of me with his gaze, and to know, before our movements swept us along, that I *wanted* to give myself to him, without mask or reservation.

I was only vaguely conscious of this intention, though I was not unaware of the erotic game to which it gave rise, the one letting herself be seen in her nakedness while the other remained the same, armed with his usual appearance. Such a difference underlined the gap between roles – taking, giving. These roles had to be distinct from the outset. But it was all so fast, and the sequence of movements that followed so simple when, naked in his turn, Julien joined me on the bed, the sexual act so disappointing. Still incapable of paying attention to our moves, so paralysed was I by the brutal break with habit and the surge of contradictory emotions, that I could see only how similar the situation was to others of the same type, not what it contained that was fundamentally new. 'That's all it is', such was my feeling when, after this first exploration of an unknown body, I found myself dressed again, ready to leave and seized by a new loneliness. For, far from feeling closer to Julien, I realised that in that instant our usual links had come untied. I did not recognise him: over the familiar image of the man that I had met so often over the past few weeks was superimposed that of a face and body that were strange to me, a memory of intimacy and behaviour that nothing had announced. Thus we are troubled, misled and disappointed by the outline of a face, the texture of a skin or the particular smell that we are breathing in for the first time, before these same elements, through the effects of habit, become the very signs by which we identify our love. If he noticed my look of sadness, like a reproach, before I had even left, if we did not experience the urgency that threw us towards each other later on, I was still able, in retrospect, to go back with emotion over the novelty of those hours of which I had been deprived by a sort of insensibility.

During the days that followed, I played and replayed in my memory the sequence of events that I had just lived through, giving myself up to the precision of Julien's movements, reliving scenes in which, devoid of reactions, I had not been able to take part at the time. I gradually became familiar with these new images of him, came to feel glad that, at last, an upheaval whose importance I had not, however, yet gauged, had occurred in my life, which had long been too quiet. I don't know to what extent this change of mind was the result of a deliberate decision on my part or if the way Julien approached love and performed its movements made me forget my taste for ethereal subtleties, for vibrations so delicate that they were indistinguishable from silence; without even being aware of it, I entered a domain rich in possibilities that resembled pleasure while going beyond it. Why would the movements I had performed with others acquire a radically new significance with him? There was no comparison between what I had felt with them and the degree of excitement to which he took me.

7

All the sensual pleasures of the earth

Several days went by before I saw Julien again; I had
arranged to spend them in the country. The silence and
stillness of my surroundings suited my state of disorientation: I felt not only as if I had been taken out of time,
which was the case whenever I went to that place enclosed
by forest, but also, having left behind my life habits, as if
I had lost the markers and boundaries that defined it. And
there in that unbroken belt of forest, in the grip of a kind
of astonishment, I continually relived the last few hours
we had spent together. From the mental confusion into
which I was plunged there soon emerged something like
regret, at having failed to appreciate the value of what he
was giving me: I had remained impervious to the happiness he wanted me to experience, for which our meetings,
like his letters, had nevertheless prepared me. True, I was
not predisposed to happiness, whereas it had long been
familiar to Julien; he had made its pursuit one of the aims
of his life as well as a discipline of mind.

Transcribed, his daily notes, to which I now returned,
would seem banal, but what love letter would not, when
read with a detached eye? To the first letters and as was

my habit, I had indeed applied my critical mind, ready to discover a search for effect that betrayed affectation and appeared to reveal a certain lack of feeling, but very quickly, subduing a mistrust that seemed petty, I had come to depend on those few sentences which, every morning, assuring me that he was thinking of me, shone a magical light upon the rest of the day; unfailingly, they conveyed the momentum of the early happy days of our love.

Julien wrote well, like those who, having had much practice in the art of letter-writing, know how to avoid the laborious, contrived or naïve feel that one often encounters; his letters, which, unlike mine, refrained from self-analysis, reflected his ability to let himself go, the spontaneity and wealth of impulses that he possessed in the highest degree in ordinary life and which never ceased to surprise me. 'One has to let oneself be carried away by happiness,' he asserted, as if it were the most natural thing in the world and, in an attempt to make the feeling universal, he claimed that at that moment in France some twenty-five million men and women were having an experience similar to ours, surrounding us in a 'sea of love'; but instead of accepting this vision, as I should have done since it was inspired by love, I answered, realistically (but who, in such a case, needs realism?), that this sea of love would be seriously threatened by the amount of misunderstandings and cruelty that exist in all human relations. This detail was proof enough, if proof were needed, of how far I still was from being able to give myself up to the powerful movement of the couple in 'The Waltz', with which everything had started.

They used words, these letters, that spoke of taking flight and of joy, of the beauty and tremor of love; like the one in which he told me he had seen a sublime Watteau, and trembled because I was not at his side, or the one in which he assured me that breathing near me was a new and exhilarating exercise (just as breathing far from me was a novel, painful exercise); and if the word exercise, used twice, confirmed that for Julien, too, the world was being renewed, since each absolutely new thing is difficult and must be learned, similarly the word 'breathing' led me to feel the reality of an opening up, an expansion of the entire being that was truly exhilarating.

But the first time we made love, that impetus was temporarily hidden, replaced by immense surprise that turned to regret. If I had sometimes had the impression of remaining on the fringes of life, or of being isolated as if under a bell jar outside which figures moved with no connection to me whatsoever, here something was now happening, life in a turbulent form was coming and the glass walls of my prison were cracking, just as the spell that kept Sleeping Beauty asleep for a hundred years was broken, or the mist holding the sorcerer's victim prisoner in the depths of the forest cleared one day; my surroundings certainly lent themselves to this: their influence, combined with the power of the images I was recalling, enabled me, by verifying the profound truth of fairy tales, to set my love affair in the context of ancient myths from which it took an additional justification and a reflection of eternity.

Back in Paris, I found a letter from him; it was enough to remove my last doubts, conveying with a force a thousand times greater the momentum that, during days of confusion, I thought I had lost. I had room within me for a single certainty – that I loved Julien – and a single wish – to see him again.

What I remembered most from the letter, which profoundly moved me, was the last few lines. 'At least accept for what it is my feeling of deep happiness . . .'; I found there too, together with the tone of his earlier letters, the spirit of the work of art that he had taken me to see and from which seemed to stem this emotion, this involvement which was quite unlike flirtatiousness and testified to the fervour with which one approached love. In the light of those lines, everything became clear, and the scenes I had lived through, ceasing to appear like a break in their suddenness, came on the contrary to take their place in the continuity of my amorous reverie.

Julien's entire life showed to what degree he had a sense of the power of love, he who devoted his time and his thoughts to it and drew his strength from it. Why, otherwise, would he have added, after the words that had so struck me: 'happiness and power of knowing you', a phrase in which I saw a concentrated expression of my own feelings? The energy that love confers, and upon which Julien drew so amply, was to irrigate every last fibre of my being; but at present, greatly increased by my recent discovery and the certainty that I had shown myself unworthy, that I had disappointed him, it inspired me with a powerful desire to see him again, to make up for being afraid, for holding back.

It was in the grip of violent emotion, as if deprived of the ability to think, that, crossing the city like a sleepwalker, I made my way to the white room where Julien was waiting for me. As soon as the door opened, I was against him, enclosed in his arms, buried in his embrace to the point of disappearing; all I had left were scraps of sentences, disconnected words, confused explanations mingling with kisses; I didn't know anything any more, I tried to explain both my coldness and the guilt from which he was to free me. But explanations no longer mattered; in his haste, he was already pulling me after him. We were simply instruments of the strange force pushing us towards each other. I had then for the first time the impression of obeying a law that went well beyond our selves. Lying on the bed, still fully dressed, I watched his face as he stood before me and removed his clothes one item at a time. Despite movements that sometimes obscured them, I saw nothing but his eyes, their expression absent, impersonal and resolute, fixed on mine. It seemed now as if time had stopped and after the feverishness of a little earlier there followed a lull, produced, though, by a tension so great that any movement had a particular impact; and I waited for the definitive move promised by his gaze, conscious that this tension must lead to it, that I had come here for this outcome alone. But Julien delayed the decisive moment, approaching me slowly, his eyes still fixed on mine. I had plenty of time to desire and imagine him, plenty of time to wait and prepare myself for him. And when he came to me, with no caress preceding it since nothing but the essential was needed, when Julien entered me, it was as if all the emptiness, all the lack and pain accumulated in me for so long were for ever abolished. As Julien increased the intensity of his presence inside me, very slowly, in a barely perceptible back-and-forth motion and always looking at me, I was aware that we were joined and that I wanted nothing else. Even if there had only been this presence and the expression in his eyes, the sensation of being filled where I had been hollow and incomplete, as I was sometimes made to feel when he paused, I would have been transported, thrown into a joy of which 'one cannot speak'. More even than the pleasure that followed, it was this moment of union, deferred, awaited, preceded by extreme tension, and become therefore inevitable, like forces that cannot be halted once unleashed, this move from suffering absence to fullness of being, in the most physical and spiritual sense of the term, that made me reach a state I had never known before. This moment, which he strove to prolong with his stillness, was one of the highest consciousness, before pleasure gradually made me lose hold. My attention was fully engaged, occupied with grasping the fact of being penetrated, with detecting the vast fundamental impulses that it stirred – the new conjunction of union and pleasure. He was inside me, nothing else mattered, I was filled by him. But soon I felt the arrival, like a breaking point, of the moment when, precisely, I would lose my awareness, where ceasing to be attentive to these movements and what was causing them, to what was taking me 'body and soul', as the expression so aptly puts it, I would let myself sink to the bottom of a darkness that resembled sleep or death. This break – this loss of soul, the moment when the entire universe was annihilated – I was waiting for it as a deliverance, but Julien's arrival had already prepared me for it, and, taking me far from this side of the world, it had raised me to another level of happiness. Perhaps I had unknowingly wished for this, because suddenly it seemed like the only essential thing, like the final outcome of a life that had been one long wait. And I marvelled that this bond of hard flesh joining our two bodies was so exactly adapted to my desire that, mysteriously, it filled an absence that I had felt to the point of anguish.

I don't know whether I tried from that moment on to find the same intensity of feeling every time – that pleasure 'superior to all the sensual pleasures of the earth' – whether I understood from that moment what some religions teach, that the union of two bodies can be a path to the liberation of the self, a way out of the incompleteness that oppresses us, an end to the 'not enough' that can afflict us our whole life. The presence of Julien inside me gave me access to another plane of being, beyond division, beyond time that defeats us and beyond the continual feeling of lack. It was the key to another world, so different to the one in which we live that, in my wish to name it and finding no suitable term, I apply to it the qualifier divine. No doubt I was tired after being patient for too long and, without knowing it, ready to fall into all the traps against which the modern day warns women (a mistrust that, in my opinion, simply limits the variety and extent of our pleasures). And then, Julien had a gift for unearthing in the very depths of beings resources of which they themselves were unaware, a capacity to suffer and to love that made all other tendencies trivial.

Sometimes, when trying to detach myself from him, I sought pleasure, no longer concerned about union, so that it would take me to those states for which I yearned, and Julien was nothing but the means of attaining them, the forgotten officiant of a ceremony that was secretly taking place for *my* benefit. True, very soon, even when I was most in love with him, I started to wonder whether, beyond love, I was not continuing a quest in which I had always been engaged. But, during those first weeks, transported by a discovery that had entirely altered the look of things, I thought only of the happiness of the hours when we were together, leading to the moment for which I came – the moment when, our bodies merging, I stopped being in the world in order, as I had once solemnly written in a bad childhood poem, 'to be, absolutely'.

The ego discourses only
when it is hurt

Often, as far as the literature of love is concerned, we have nothing but a long succession of tears and sighs, or the observation of a humiliating obsession that reduces the lover to a slave. But what of all the rest, which exists all the same, in other words the moments of happiness? 'Fulfilments: they are not spoken,' states Roland Barthes, 'so that erroneously, the amorous relation seems reduced to a long complaint. This is because, if it is inconsistent to express suffering badly, on the other hand, with regard to happiness, it would seem culpable to spoil its expression: the ego discourses only when it is hurt; when I am fulfilled, or remember having been so, language seems pusillanimous: I am transported, *beyond language.'*

Must one then resign oneself to describing only the complaint, without trying to convey a little of the joy through which 'man is reduced to nothing'? Yet it is essential to convey this happiness, in part at least, even if it means spoiling its expression, chipping a corner off its inexpressible reality.

8

The loss of the self

If I were to choose from the moments of happiness I have experienced, I think I would go back to certain periods of my adolescence spent in the country. Not that I was terribly happy then, but because there were instants, quite unrelated to the rest of my life, whose link with the experience of love I would later come to understand. Such moments, as I have already mentioned, have haunted my existence: compared to them, it seemed like a flat dreary expanse, deserted as far as the eye could see; only a flaw in my make-up, I thought, prevented me from seeing its contrasts and its interest. They left me a memory of having reached another plane of being and, for a long time, I had a burning, painful desire to return there. As well as a need to succeed in finding a similar state, I had an unbearable sense of my own powerlessness.

How far back did my awareness of such singular moments go? During a period of my life, that of my earliest youth when I spent the summer months in the country, they were frequent and, as it were, spontaneous. All I had to do, leaving the house and its bustle, was to enter the wood, dense and still at that time of year, and I would feel overcome by foreknowledge of another world. A strange stagnation reigned there, animated only by the buzzing of flies, and the sound itself, unceasing and monotonous, redolent with heat and laziness, contributed to the impression that one had stepped outside time. As far as the eye could see I was surrounded by the green shade of oak trees, pierced here and there by a ray of sun landing on the sandy path or on the leaning tips of tall ferns in the undergrowth, drawing islands of light in which insects whirled. The well-being that I felt was like drowsiness, a happy stupor that took me away from myself; the hours that had gone before, the days and the years and the person that I was were all forgotten, only this indefinitely prolonged minute, in which I gradually felt myself disappear, was real.

But when I could not go beyond it, I knew that this state, which was the product of a vague sensual satisfaction and which brought me a sort of peace, had failed in its aim. For, having achieved happiness of a different kind, I expected something quite else from it than this imperceptible slide, like the loss of consciousness on the edge of sleep, or the trance into which one is sometimes plunged by the mere presence of the loved one – that miring of one's entire being, that happy inability to react or even feel. I had noticed that it was most often just when, focusing my attention on some detail, I became absorbed by it that the transition to the 'intensified vision' came. Very slowly a leaf fell, the branch of a tree imperceptibly shook: all I needed was this leading thread to pull me out of myself

43

and to prepare me, like the poet Marvell in the grip of ecstasy in 'The Garden', for taking longer flight, for being at one with the leaf I was gazing at, with the branch that bore it, with the forest as a whole – for an outpouring of my entire being beyond its boundaries. I *was* the leaf, just as it was me, all sense of separateness was removed.

I had similar experiences later, but never with the intensity that characterised them during that period. I believe that sight is the favoured means of access to such states: I have sometimes stared at a form until I have lost all awareness that I am looking, forgetting myself in the object of my gaze which then appears, like a revelation, in its uniqueness, freed from the drab appearance in which habit has cloaked it. By some spell, the world had ceased to be invisible, it was no longer a faded decor, it was *alive*. Later, when I started drawing classes and spent hours concentrating on a form so as to capture it *from the inside*, I realised that these states were occurring more frequently and lasting longer; when I was walking in the street I became aware of contours, masses, rhythms and colours, and I wished for no riches other than those, no happiness other than being thus present in the world, than *seeing*. But it was something quite different to the simple action of looking, as I later bitterly experienced when, despite my efforts, I fell from the state of being a seer back to trudging through the humdrum, when the force of gravity once more weighed me down.

Between such hours and normal routine there was the

same difference as between life and a state of insensibility. To what could one attribute the sudden transition from being only semi-present in life, which was my usual perception, to an altered vision of reality? It was as if my senses, usually asleep, had for a few moments recovered their power, and the landscape had suddenly gone from being external, detached and distant, to being present to the point of inhabiting me. Later, my reading enabling me to examine in greater depth and analyse what I had at the time only experienced, I used the words opaqueness and transparency and was tempted, following the intuition I had had, to see it as a form of knowledge. For the limitations that define and trap us, the state of division in which we live, occupied, harassed, obsessed by a thousand trivial thoughts that anchor us at a precise moment in time and in society, all of this is erased at such moments, just as a wall that was blocking our view collapses, returning us to our first feeling of unity. As I was to learn, love also provided us with the means for this emergence.

Indeed, at first sight, the experience of fusion that I had in the woods and the happiness attained in love had little in common. These brief moments of life suffused with light, enveloped in inner silence, as evoked by certain tranquil images, such as Vermeer's *Woman with a Water Jug* fixed in an unchanging present, did not resemble the violent agitation into which I had been thrown by the fact of loving; they were even, apparently, quite the opposite. For they had led to a vision that seemed to go well beyond the sensual, approaching rather, for the reader of Blake that I was, the imaginative vision. But going back, long after Julien and I had separated, over an experience whose power had not ceased to impose itself upon me, I began to sense what it was that linked states that seemed so different. But it was not surprising that the essential revelation of my adolescence, which seemed to betray a predisposition towards mystical states, should re-emerge in this fundamental liaison, in the love that, so belatedly, I was experiencing. What I had long sought, but without finding the path, not thinking that love might be it, was perhaps – rather than going deeper into an intuition – to rekindle the happiness that accompanied it. And, if I analysed it, I sensed that this happiness stemmed from a sudden liberation of the being as it escaped its isolation and came into contact with another reality. The nature of that reality mattered little, as long as it was limitless (only later would I try to imagine it). I have wondered whether the pleasure brought by love, like the pleasure one feels in the middle of a landscape, does not consist of the shattering of the limits that define us, whether loving is not freeing oneself from the narrowness of such limits in order to *merge*, to connect with a deep current of life which, joining us to the other or to the world, has the power to take us from ourselves, to carry us very far from ourselves. Was the feeling of liberation that I experienced long ago in a landscape by observing a leaf on a tree, not the same one that had, again, struck me in love when I merged with Julien

– but in that case with an intensity that owed nothing to the will – and could I not from then on identify it as the pleasure experienced in the loss of self?

9

Praise of vertigo

Was it the day after that extraordinary afternoon that Julien invited me for a walk in one of the large forests that edge Paris? We arranged to meet at my flat and go from there to the rose garden in this forest, a place he particularly loved. Always, he was concerned to link the moments we spent together with a sight that I would remember. Just as he endeavoured to put his life in harmony with the works of art with which he surrounded himself, imbuing his days with their influence, either, prompted by a sudden impulse, by going to a museum where a painting of singular power awaited him, or by buying a delicately bound book that he spent a long time admiring, so he placed the emotion he derived from such moments at the centre of his relations with others. Much more than aesthetic pleasure, these daily encounters were a vital need for Julien: they were the means of transmuting familiar details into objects of surprise, the small change of life into fairy gold. Of course this was not the vocabulary he would have chosen: in his view, it was less a question of transmutation than a certain quality of the gaze one casts on reality; his was constantly recharged by encountering art and beauty in their most diverse forms. I would go so far as to say that such works were his fundamental preoccupation, a source of energy as well as his profession; if he could not, as the well-known phrase goes, turn his 'life into art', then at least he would apply himself to making art the foundation of his life. Julien experienced a body's sensuality just as much before a reproduction of *Susanna and the Elders* by Rembrandt, as in the presence of one of his mistresses naked. In his mind, the almost impersonal tenderness, that he felt for the body thus offered up to his gaze, was linked to his admiration for the artist's picture – for the expressive power of the brushstroke which, hitching up the cloth, uncovered the full solid thighs of a servant girl. This diffuse eroticism underlay his relationship with the world; his sense of poetry and attraction to living beings were based on it. Moreover, Julien knew its power so well that he had devoted his life to sex and love. How struck I was, in one of our earliest conversations, when he admitted to his love of bodies, of all possible bodies, of the bodies laid out on the beach in which, every summer, he delighted in discovering such a great life force, when to my eyes, not filled with a poetic vision but prosaic reality, they were, spread-eagled on the sand and gleaming with suntan oil, a somewhat revolting sight, let's be honest.

The next day, he wanted therefore to show me the roses that were just coming into flower, not the frothy round-faced flowers whose excessive blooming I loved, but roses of a more ancient type, slight, discreet flowers whose stems, with their large red, sail-shaped thorns, he particularly liked. By chance, the weather was good. We walked past café terraces where people were still sitting at their tables in the sun after lunch, terraces that I had passed every day, conscious only of the looks of indifference or boredom that people sitting cast at passers-by. But that day I saw neither the tables nor the people around them; I was surrounded by a haze of sun and colour in which all I could distinguish was Julien's face, all I could hear was his voice; his mere presence had plunged me into a state that reduced the outside world to nothing. Of the taxi ride to the park, I remember only a few details, but they must have been indelibly impressed on my memory because they still appear to me today with the surreal clarity of certain images in dreams; all of them relate to him: despite his show of cheerfulness, a look of absence, at times, combined with anxiety, a slight tiredness denoted by the crease at the corners of his mouth; if they troubled me when I remembered them later, at the time they only sharpened my desire for him – the desire to reach the unknown in him that escaped me. This was to be the most powerful stimulus to a love that was profoundly physical: holding his face, inscrutable and revealed, allowed me to believe that I was grasping in a single movement a mystery that was to my eyes unfathomable.

Neither the roses, though he pointed out their names, written on little labels, with the date they were named, nor the shady paths along which we walked could capture my attention: of that afternoon spent at his side, of that perfect garden in full bloom, I noticed nothing; all that remains in my memory is a bubble of iridescent light, out of time, in which for a moment I found myself isolated with him. On the way back, behind one of the park hedges, he took me in his arms; that day, no other gesture united us; he knew that desire thus curbed, mastered, is increased a hundredfold and that the mere proximity of our bodies would plunge us into a state often described as vertigo or intoxication, because it does indeed remove our usual reference points (but wine, which, on the contrary, sank me into a kind of lethargy, never gave me that feeling of elation, of lightness). In the métro on the way back into Paris, aware once more of the crowd around us, I wondered whether our state could be read on our faces, whether a happy radiance did not emanate from us visibly, palpably almost, like the halo that sets apart the chosen in paintings of saints; it must have been a strange sight, a couple in middle age, alone amidst the throng, with such an air of absence on their faces.

I may never have been as happy again as I was during that walk and the hours that followed. The feeling of loneliness that sometimes followed love, the return to awareness of a distance that kills, was replaced by a soaring of the self, a condition where nothing can reach it any more, neither accident, nor fear, nor change. Love had risen in me to such a level that not the slightest flaw, not the slightest gap remained through which thought, doubt or worry might enter: and being thus filled with love, without the object of that feeling even mattering, without desire for him troubling me, so fulfilled was I by his presence in me, I felt that I was lifted off the ground, 'transported', 'ravished', as one can be ravished away from one's loved ones, one's family or oneself – since language readily uses for love the vocabulary of war.

By luck I was spending the evening alone; I would in any case have found it impossible to cope with an ordinary conversation, to find my footing again in daily life. I remained in a state of dazzled absence for a long time, and others, myself, familiar objects, all seemed transformed, both close and distant, as if they had undergone a metamorphosis during a long journey, as if they had become unfamiliar and I was seeing them for the first time. They existed in another world, a world that I no longer inhabited.

During this period of our relationship, after particularly powerful moments of happiness when, walking with Julien, I was again overcome by the strange disturbance into which his presence inevitably threw me, I experienced those peculiar states of weightlessness in which one seems to be floating rather than walking. And I recalled baroque statues, their elongated bodies, with their markedly lopsided stance, one knee bent as if about to take a dance step, arms outstretched and turning improbably, stretching, extending, rising, an irrepressible movement running through them to the tip of the finger that they point up at the sky: they proclaimed a state of lightness, the irresistible impulse which, as it did me, released them from the force of gravity and swept them upwards. When I discovered these statues, their frenzy seemed excessive and their attitude closer to theatricality than true spirituality, but today I was struck on the contrary by how right their movement seemed: the twist imprinted on their bodies arose from a happiness that they could no longer contain. Sounds reached me only muffled, as if the luminous bubble that isolated us in the rose garden had re-formed around us and, of the sights in the street, I perceived only patches of colour, not details or shapes, even though at certain moments I forced myself to focus my attention on the face of some passer-by, as one decides in a boat to drop anchor so as to check how far one has drifted. The world now seemed very far away, as if seen through the wrong end of a telescope, filled with people who lacked an essential dimension – the dimension that Julien's existence granted me; an essential joy – the joy of loving him. It was a world that was nothing to me, since it did not revolve around Julien, but I looked upon it with the tolerance granted by the certainty of possessing an incalculable advantage over others.

I don't know if he experienced these changes in the current of life to the same extent; we continued to write to each other, on a daily basis, whereas our meetings remained infrequent. But, unlike my letters, which described my inner adventure to him, his evoked no notable change or surprising discoveries made in the grip of a new feeling: Julien experienced this love with serenity, for me it was an endless upheaval.

During those first weeks, as if emerging from long seclusion, I was occupied with unfurling my whole being, opening myself up fold by fold in a continual desire to receive him.

10

Distances

Not long afterwards, I went to London to attend a conference. I was not sorry to be going; it gave me an opportunity to catch my breath far from Julien and foreshadowed the escapes by which I would run away from the exhausting tension.

This time I travelled by boat, leaving Paris early in the morning. A sea crossing, the view of the expanse of water, a long day spent in a state of vacancy, it all seemed conducive to a much-needed rest. I wished simply to let myself go, before my mind returned endlessly to the only subject that had occupied it for the last two months.

The day before my departure a troubling episode occurred. That evening, Julien was to chair a round table bringing together a number of academics and experts from the art world; on this occasion, as always in such cases, books by the participants would be set out in display cabinets in the entrance hall of the library where the debate was taking place. At his request, I came to see him preside over a discussion to which he attached importance. It was the first time that, emerging from our private world, I had dared meet him in public, on an occasion relating to his work. I was delighted with a situation where I would have the opportunity to watch him without him seeing me, without being distracted from him by an awareness of his gaze or by the words he was speaking to me. And yet I was somewhat fearful of this evening: would it not represent a discrepancy, an uncomfortable change of scene or, worse still, the risk of seeing him in a new light, of discovering a side of him that I did not know – a side that would reveal a section of his life away from me, far from me, in which I was not included and of which, perhaps from fear that I might start to imagine this life, I wanted to know nothing? But even before I had had a chance to catch sight of him in the crowd, the discrepancy occurred in a way that was unpredictable and even more troubling than I had foreseen. In a display case, one of his books was open at the dedication page. What I read there plunged me into an uneasiness whose cause I was quite unable to identify at the time: the words I read were almost exactly the same ones he had written to me a little while ago in one of his precious notes; but this time they were not addressed to me. Not that they were about love, they were in fact two, maybe three words evoking spring, the season when we met, but suddenly Julien was no longer the same, he was no longer the person who, like me, lived exclusively for our love: he mass-produced notes and dedications, making the most of inspirations prompted by the desire to please everyone, not by the love of a single person. This feeling of strangeness stifled all other feelings as I watched him show off at the rostrum, no longer recognising him: it was not a matter of betrayal, but of seriously failing love, as my demanding nature defined it. My memory of that evening was one of unreality: I had lost Julien when he was right before my eyes; the person I could see was an impostor, a fraud, I could not reconcile the sight of him with the image that survived in me. When, at the end of the discussion, I approached this stranger to congratulate him, all I could do was mumble a few words and refuse his invitation to join them for dinner, him and his friends. I fled without further explanation to put an end to the nightmare.

This was my foretaste of hell: being together yet divided, farther apart than if there was an ocean between us, for one can cross a distance in space, but nothing, no means in the world, seemed able to bridge this one, which was of the mind. This was, especially, the first warning sign – even if I'd already had an intuition of the difference that existed between us – the precursor of a suffering with which I would have to come to terms. Our meeting had not caused him a shock, it was not the unique experience upon which everything else converged, but it came to take its place amongst the other emotions of a life harmoniously devoted to love and seduction. However hard I might strive to do so, there could be no question of keeping Julien, immobilising him. I would soon have this foreboding confirmed. So began my long apprenticeship, during which the torments and benefits entailed by such a discrepancy between modes of love would be revealed to me. But for the time being we were at that happy stage of passion where one needs to love in unison, to check at every moment that one is moved by the same impulses. I had no sooner fallen into a difficult sleep broken by dreams when the telephone rang: taking leave of his friends, Julien wanted to know what I had thought of the evening, to make sure we would be meeting the following morning, very early, before I left, and the impatience in his voice, its vibration and gentleness, the way he pronounced the words of tenderness that I would feast on for days, suddenly dispelled my earlier fears. It was also the first of the sudden reversals at which he excelled and which launched me from despondency into joy.

I stayed in London only for a few days. I was pleased to be there at that time of year: spring had a particular charm there, it unfurled with more brightness, momentum and intimacy than in any other city. Often, watching out for the appearance of the first buds on the trees, I had felt bereft, as if guilty of my exhaustion – of having nothing in me that might respond to that renewed vitality, nothing but a feeling of sterility in the face of a rebirth that reached even the smallest branch. It certainly gave me pleasure, but this vague feeling seemed inadequate compared to what the occasion required: the force of the explosion after months of dreary waiting in which I remained indefinitely trapped; it was like attending festivities from which, due to an inexplicable difference, I remained excluded. Life was there, but it was out of reach. Yet this time I had the feeling of a new dawn powerful enough to match the flawless blue, the festive trees, the freshness of the leaves, all the movement of life resuming. The streets that I knew well, the gardens and squares that I had walked round so many times, I saw them all with new eyes. The flowers had a new radiance, the grass was a tender green, the air was perfectly limpid, the softness of the distant shades of green in the parks transmitted a happiness that I had been too absorbed to feel in Paris. Far from Julien, in peace and quiet, I could at last think about him, without waiting for the telephone call or letter on which my life hung.

I had noticed that his absence, paradoxically, restored a presence of which the excess of emotion sometimes deprived me when we were together: then, I was no longer conscious of him or my happiness, stripped of the ability to think, in a sort of trance; or, sometimes, he retained the mood of the moment preceding our meeting, he was agitated or despondent, he assumed one of the facets of a multiple personality, but in that guise, as familiar as he was to me, I could not find Julien in his entirety, could not grasp the being that he was beyond these successive incarnations. I was left at a loss, near him and yet separate from him. The intensity of my desire removed my ability to enjoy his presence.

And so it happens, in our relations with others, that we lose them when they are still by our side, a gap suddenly appearing between the way we see them and what they reveal to us. Absence corrects this distance, restoring our usual perception and our feelings of liking or friendship: it enables us to see them as a whole rather than noticing a specific trait that annoys, irritates or disappoints us, and occupies our mind to the exclusion of everything else.

I tried to picture his features. Always, it was the same expression that returned to my memory, that pensive air, absorbed in his own thoughts, eyes half-closed, and the thickness of his mouth where I detected, the first time I saw him, such appetite and such weariness, the crease at the corners revealing his dissatisfaction at the time. In my eyes, that expression was like Julien's true self showing through and, because I could see in it both temptation and wrenching pain, I liked it more than all the others; no doubt it betrayed his vulnerability, an immense need to be re-assured but – I was not mistaken here – it also indicated a need to withdraw into himself, to preserve his solitude. So I sought the other expression, which did not contradict this wish but softened its affirmation, the one where, roaring with laughter, he revealed, together with the slight gap between his teeth (I loved that gap too), a need for both pleasure and sharing. But this expression could not, any more than the other, reassure me for long, since he revealed himself only to change the next moment. Was it this mobility, the continual movement, the constant contra-dictions that made pleasure and anxiety alternate on his face with which I fell in love, was it with the weariness that, sometimes, froze him like a mask, when the momentum of life and the work of death cancelled each other out (did he not assume life fully, taking it head-on, seeking it where it was most intense)? I don't know. None of these reasons made much sense. The feeling that gripped me had nothing to do with Julien's qualities or faults: it was beyond measure as it was beyond analysis, being imprinted on the deepest part of me, on my physical being, which is inseparable from my spiritual being.

Even if I had stopped believing in him fully, I would still have continued loving him for a single one of his intonations, a single one of his gestures. In other words, my judgment had to submit to my love, which was biased towards adoration supported by carnal passion.

Thus, leaving a landscape that was entirely organised around him to adopt the point of view of an outside observer, I went back over the origins of this love and wondered about its cause, marvelling that from tiny details, such as the curve of his lips, a feeling of such magnitude could have arisen. What could the link be between a certain movement of his hand – the way he smoothed a book cover, for instance – and the devotion that the gesture inspired in me, a devotion so great that it filled space, stifling any vague feeling of resistance, making of me his creature? Yet, it was from similar fragments that I received him; it was from them that I recognised him; they were like the manifested sign of his true being, the guarantee that he was him and that the love that swept over me was not mistaken. His body, his movements, his attitudes could not lie to me, and if his successive moods sometimes disconcerted me, if, I felt, they expressed him only imperfectly, a shape at least, a feature, a movement, however fleeting, however imperceptible, suddenly catching my eye, restored Julien to me in his entirety. One day, I remember, after a longer separation than the others, when I had made the decision to create some distance between us, he came to see me with the obvious aim of winning me back. It wasn't his words that convinced me, I had prepared myself to confront them and fight them, but a forgotten detail, the shape of his little finger, slightly curved outwards, which gave something ethereal to the movement of his hand, which I suddenly noticed as I was watching him, causing a flood of memories – held at a distance until then – to surge back into my mind, and I found myself without strength, unable to resist the tenderness that was sweeping over me, devoid of any will: better than any argument, the unexpected sight of that detail struck at my heart. What a strange feeling, that of dissolving, of no longer being able to rally one's thoughts or one's energy, as if life were gradually ebbing away. Powerless, sunk into a kind of torpor, one is attending a surrender that is only half consented to – desire taking hold of a person once more.

I could not doubt the power of this desire. If I was, at the time, nowhere near grasping the thousand ways in which Julien managed to intensify it – more than a deliberate game, it was an instinctive skill, a tendency in his nature — I had, at least, such great faith in this skill that I left it up to him, soon discovering what I did not yet know about myself.

Hypnosis

Hens are good subjects for hypnosis: you simply put their heads under their wings, as I was taught in my country childhood, whirl them around energetically, and they remain there as if asleep.

Going through A Lover's Discourse, *I found this description of a method that was undoubtedly slightly different, but apparently produced the same result. The comparison drawn between the hen and the lover was what interested me most.*

'I am nothing more than the Jesuit Athanasius Kircher's wonderful hen: feet tied, the hen went to sleep with her eyes fixed on the chalk line which, like a binding, was traced not far from her beak; when she was untied, she remained motionless, fascinated, "submitting to her vanquisher', as the Jesuit says (1646).'

It is not always enough, far from it, to receive, like the hen, a little tap on the wing for the lover to wake from the state of enchantment into which he has been plunged and resume the normal course of his activities, as if nothing had happened. The hen shook herself and began pecking again, forgetting all about the preceding episode.

The stages both the hen and the lover go through have, however, strong similarities.

11

The first time

Free of Julien's influence, I allowed myself to go back over our first time (I had decided to ignore the time before) and to relive it as it unfolded. The haste with which he seized me and led me to the bed, then, by contrast, the slowness of his movements as he undressed me, and his gaze, that seemed inhabited, which did not leave mine, my impression (though it remained confused) of being caught in a ceremony in which we were merely the celebrants, the moment, which I had plenty of time to await and imagine, when I felt him, neither timid nor imperious, but powerful, undeniable, enter me. Then, I was without thought, or memory, or limit. His eyes remained fixed on mine, holding me until the instant when I would let myself go, observing the pleasure intensifying as he moved. Our faces so close, and our breaths mingled, and, from time to time, he stopped all movement so that our union was all that we were aware of: I was in him as he was in me. This time, until the moment of pleasure, the awareness did not leave us for a second. Later on, he chose sometimes to forget me, plunging into me as if into the night or the sea, to lose himself; I saw his eyes, above me, no longer on a level with mine, their impersonal gaze seemingly fixed on an invisible point in space; sometimes too, briefly, the way one calls out to someone, he said my name as if to remind me that, as far away as he was, he had not left me completely. More than ever, I felt then that, beyond my person, Julien was seeking love, partaking of a mystery that went beyond us both. Back from these descents into pleasure, he lavished signs of tenderness upon me, as one can upon someone with whom one has shared an experience at the very edge, and this tenderness, I felt, though directed at me, went well beyond me – to life, to the body that held that life within it, to the love with which it was charged. We held each other closely, learning through our caresses to know, to feel from our fingertips to our hearts, the curves, forms, hollows and contours, and sweetness of the other's body. I remember that I tried to describe my sense of discovery to him that day: there was not an inch of his body that remained unknown to me, not an inch that I did not welcome and accept in an act of love, and not a particle of my own body that did not open up to him, offering itself in a consent in which I found fulfilment. 'For that alone,' he told me, 'for a single time like this, one should always be grateful, whatever happens later.' Why, when I had loved and known physical love before, did that time seem like the first, as if only today had I become fully conscious – but conscious in body as much as in mind – of the act performed? Nothing of what I had felt until then counted, I told myself ungratefully, the times before had been merely attempts leading me to this peak, but to which they bore no relation; like knowledge recently imprinted on each of my cells, a new landscape suddenly appeared before me.

12

Reading

Was it at this stage in our affair, or later, when other scenes had become superimposed upon this one, that I started to gauge the extent of my discoveries? The world was revealed in a new light and, anxious to understand as much as to feel, since this was a way of deepening my love and possessing it more, I tried to analyse what was happening to me, linking a feeling that was so new to the great thoughts on love that I had flirted with and to which I decided to return: so I threw myself into reading a variety of works, by classical rather than recent authors, true – contemporary systems have attached little importance to the subject – and I came to the source to which one sooner or later returns, Plato's *Banquet*, a text that I found profoundly boring during my student years, rediscovered later when reading the English Romantic poets, and whose full meaning was only now becoming apparent: does he not make of eroticism the vital impulse that enables one to contemplate the eternal forms and to partake of the essence? Does he not grant it a role and dignity denied it by the Christian religion, whose insistence on procreation as the purpose of love had always put me off?

I was very careful, however, not to share my thoughts with Julien, knowing that, though interested in watching me develop under his influence, he did not like the work of introspection that I was in the habit of engaging in, nor the analysis which, in his view, deprived things of their spontaneity and mystery. From the very first long letter I wrote to him, setting out the changes that were taking place within me, he gently mocked my over-indulgence in abstraction and frequent use of 'big' words, such as soul, nowadays so unfashionable (was not my name, Camille, itself old-fashioned, an indication that I did not quite belong to an end of century where matters of sex, simplified and detached from any former context, indeed involved using the vocabulary of anatomy rather than that of spirituality?).

Ideas attracted him less than 'reality', one of his favourite words (albeit, a reality touched by a poetic vision). So from then on I tried to adapt my vocabulary to his, to express myself in concrete terms when describing my feelings, and this willingness to keep to ordinary, simple, immediate matters – what we see, feel, experience – contributed without doubt to preserving at every one of our meetings the element of silence and secrecy that is at the heart of any intensely physical love. We never engaged in any discussions of ideas, our minds never confronted each other; in truth, we spoke little of our selves or our attachment. I made my discoveries alone, even if he was their originator (and here again, despite myself, I joined the Platonic lover whose path is essentially solitary). Thus our meetings, like ceremonies determined by a religion, were invariably dedicated to love: their very infrequency, the waiting and tension that preceded them were already preparing for the moment in which they culminated – the moment towards which the rest of my life stretched, either anticipated or endlessly relived in memory.

Reflecting on it again at a distance, I understand better the spirit that drove Julien and the progress he helped me to make in the art of love. I understand better why actions that with others had had so little significance, to the extent that I had instantly forgotten them, had assumed such great significance with him. What was it, in this first scene that I was now reliving, that had endowed his movements with religious gravity? How had they differed from any other act of procreation and why did they seem so far removed from those prompted by licentiousness? It was because he had performed them like a rite, so that the act of love had become suggestive of love itself. The difference was the same, I felt, as the one that exists between the representation of a nude, of such-and-such a body captured in all its particular characteristics, and those primitive figures, gods or goddesses of love or fertility, whose curves or phallus are supposed to embody Eros in its entirety. A number of clues reveal that we are in the presence not of the individual feature, but of the sign. Another comparison, also connected to the religious, came to mind. In the liturgy, simple gestures acquire a sacred nature because we attribute a symbolic value to them: similarly in love, the intention alters the meaning and impact of the movements performed. By the spirit in which Julien was acting, leaving aside the banal episode of coupling, one amongst so many others, or perhaps choosing to accept all of these couplings, as they took place at every moment on the planet, he had, in the act of love, connected with the very essence of love. We had left the narrow realm of the particular and entered that of the general – of an elemental mystery, as it had inspired so many primitive works of art where eroticism meets the sacred. He had introduced me to the mystery through all sorts of indications, by the sudden change from haste to slowness when the time came to undress, by his impersonal, distant look while he was doing so, by the very roles that he had assigned to us, corresponding to the age-old submission of the woman to the man – I lay before him while he, standing, looked down on me – by the growing tension that he used so carefully before the event, like that which, for believers, precedes the consecration during Mass, I said to myself, recovering ancient memories and an old inner experience. But the desire that I knew he had, to reach all bodies through one single body, and to love them, also influenced my impression. I wasn't surprised that, according to the concept of the Platonic Eros, this stage was thought superior to the one that consisted in loving only one body. One must understand, writes Plato, that 'the beauty residing in such and such a body is sister to the beauty that resides in another, and that, if one must pursue the beautiful in a form perceptible to the senses, it is unparalleled folly not to judge the beauty residing in all bodies as one and the same: a thought that should make him a lover of all beautiful bodies and lessen the impetuousness of his love for a single person.' I read this passage with interest, for if I replaced the word 'beauty' with the word 'life' – a right I took since, in Julien's eyes, any manifestation of life was intrinsically beautiful and moving – it described very precisely Julien's approach to love. The end of the sentence, in particular, struck me, for it disregarded the feelings of the other, the desire for possession as well as fidelity in love, granting the lover full freedom. And, indeed, we never questioned this freedom: it was taken for granted, as was our silence on the subject (indeed, what right do we have to take another's freedom for our own advantage, preventing them from existing apart from us, and by that, from developing, evolving, living?).

13

Silence

From the start of our relationship, silence was the tacit and freely agreed rule. But if, in the early days of love, I found it easy to observe, having no specific reason to suspect that Julien was unfaithful to me, later on I came to wonder whether knowing wouldn't be less painful than imagining. At first, I took account only of the hours spent together, my love delighting in them as if they were a favour. His time belonged to me, I felt: the time that escaped me did not exist, since I could not imagine it. It seemed that the hours when we met should eclipse everything else, consigning it to the void. But, gradually, I realised that it was not so, that those other hours existed too, that they could bring him to me or take him away, and I started to wonder with obsessive curiosity about all the moments that Julien spent without me, all the days when he did not meet me, which were so much more numerous than those when he did. If love, in the words of Proust, whom I was re-reading, 'in its painful anxiety as in its happy desire, demands a totality', then I gauged the extent of the suffering implied by my consenting to a freedom which I nevertheless saw as its essential condition. But I was never prepared to question Julien about the days when we were not together, about the places where he was far from me, about the other lives in which perhaps he didn't think about me, where he was happy apart from me, without me. This was not the basis – that of wrenching pain into which one sinks, that of a possessiveness that was excessive, since it wanted to make a prisoner of a free being – on which I wanted to experience our relationship, even if I was in the grip of all the contradictory impulses, all the tormenting thoughts that assail one in such circumstances.

Either out of a concern for honesty, or a refusal to live with lies which, had they accumulated, could have destroyed him, or perhaps out of flirtatiousness, with the slight sadism that soon came to characterise our relation-ship, Julien gave me to understand that I was not the only woman in his life. For a long time I wondered about the reason for confessions that were only hinted at, never backed up, slipped as if inadvertently into the conversa-tion and which, because they were not accompanied by any specific information, left me painfully uncertain, free to ignore what I could not know, free, also, to gather the clues that the caprices of his life or his desires happened to provide during the hours we spent together. I asked myself if these half-confessions were prompted by a burst of frankness, by the need to jettison a moral weight that was too heavy, or – as I secretly hoped, because it would mean that it was a manoeuvre linked to our love – by the desire to test his power by making me suffer a little, a banal seducer's manoeuvre. His strategy was so clever, and his insinuations so subtle, that it was difficult to detect the truth, or even to know whether the affairs thus evoked were real or imaginary, from the present or past, and, especially, how much they mattered. But we had got into the habit of secrecy (to what extent was our love fed by the secrecy, by the absences, by what we kept to ourselves or merely suggested?). His freedom, if not mine, lay in what was unsaid (true, at this stage of our love, soon after vowing that such excursions would remain brief, I ceased defending a freedom which, in my better moments, seemed no more than an insipid state). It was the means of achieving the greatest intensity.

Julien assured me of his love, choosing to ignore the dismay into which I was sometimes thrown by a quick reference, made as if in passing, to a life that was hectic, rich in emotions – he did not specify what kind – in which I had no part; and he quite simply passed over in silence the unhappiness into which I was plunged by the fact of not seeing him for days. I wanted to confine myself to these assurances; only the unequalled moments, beyond all limits, should count, their novelty maintained by the very freedom that caused me pain, by the impulses that it authorised and the tensions it created. Alas, I was not always able to keep such sensible resolutions, or obey such lofty intentions; had I managed it, I might have spared myself much suffering.

Julien sought the beauty of bodies, of course, but in his

eyes this beauty was only partly linked to external forms: it was the beauty of life that moved him – such as existed in the multiplicity of bodies, imparting gestures and expressions to them; the life that initially surges, gushes forth, bursts out in its exuberance, then slowly subsides and ebbs, leaving signs of its weariness. Also, whether they were young and beautiful, or already marked by age, women always stood a chance of attracting him: a line, a wrinkle, a slightly dark shadow touched him maybe more than a smooth, young face, because he saw in it yet another effect of life. I should have been pleased by such a tendency, since I stood a good chance too, I, whom age was beginning to affect, and it would indeed have reassured me had it not implied that Julien's need to seduce was limitless. I had to reconcile myself to the fact that his aptitude to be attracted by life in all its aspects, and not just as it was concentrated in one person chosen to the exclusion of all others, 'lessened the impetuousness' of his love, in Plato's words; there could be no doubt that this was the cause of the tranquillity with which Julien loved.

Why did he remind me in love of ancient priests, their gaze lost in the distance, whose lips serenely revealed the importance of the rite they were celebrating? Indeed, at first this impression only vaguely crossed my mind. Gradually, though, I tried to analyse the reality it concealed. Julien always greeted me with the same emotion; every one of his movements betrayed an awareness of the moment towards which we infallibly slid, but when we were at our closest I saw the grave absent air on his face that I now attributed to an inner distance rather than to extreme tension: I was doubtlessly the prime cause of his emotion, but – instinctively, I understood this – it was directed too, or perhaps above all, at the hours we would be spending together, at the love that was in us, at the wonder of living in this world and loving. He lent himself to my desire with tenderness, playing the part required in our intimate celebration, whereas I passionately wanted to be possessed by him, I cared about nothing else. I quickly realised that the key to our relationship, to the pain that it contained, to the fact that for a long time it lost none of its force, lay in this gap – in the *detachment* that I found in him, so different from my own *attachment* to things being accomplished. Something in him would always remain beyond my reach, and that which eluded me was of the order of the essential. Had he not one day declared that he would like to have a limitless fund of love from which everyone could draw as they wished? Immoderation, in life, in love, this was what his whole being strove towards, beyond the person loved who was, in a way, no more than a channel, a means of access.

Of course, this discovery, while stimulating my love, was to cause me pain. Julien no doubt loved me, and he told me so, not stinting, when we saw each other, on the 'I love yous', words to which I returned endlessly, adding the murmur of his voice, and which I carried within me like a precious asset, waiting for the moment when he would consent to say them again. But he did not love me with the same absolute love that I felt for him. He tried simply to follow me with a willingness that I should have found touching. For he, who had one day confessed to having known so many women, he, who had made them discover 'unknown regions of themselves', he told me – and I readily believed him – was more often than not excluded from the frenzy he had caused. In the early days of our love, once the pleasure of conquest was past, what he loved most in me perhaps was the fervour with which I loved him. I've often wondered if his own feeling was not like a reflection of the pleasure that he detected on my face in love – the radiance of which he said that it alone was enough to make him happy. Sometimes, I felt, he summoned up all his energy so as not to be inferior to what I expected of him. And the thought dismayed me when it should have filled my heart with gratitude. Though in truth, it did to some extent, for I knew I owed to his tenderness, to his respect for love, attentions that I could not attribute to a passion as violent, as exclusive as mine.

I love you

'Once the first avowal has been made, "I love you" no longer has any meaning.' But Barthes' proof, a little too syntactic for my taste, did not convince me ('I-love-you is not a sentence . . . It is a holophrase.' It was at this point that his reasoning stopped reaching me). To me, I-love-you was not the magical, mythical word that would change me for ever: Pelleas dies on hearing Melisande say it and Beauty transforms the Beast into a Prince Charming by pronouncing it. It did not, unfortunately, have such decisive power over me. My doubts survived. I understood Barthes better when he added: 'I-love-you is without nuance. It suppresses explanations, adjustments, degrees, scruples.'

Explanations and adjustments, all things that indeed needed to be suppressed. By saying 'I love you' to me, Julien was certainly giving in to impulse, to a moment of euphoria, but he was also putting forward a definitive answer to my fears, to the questions I wanted to ask. Once the moment of joy that followed those words was over, I was tempted to think that 'I love you' was a way of keeping me quiet. There is no comeback to such a statement: it is both the end and the beginning, you cannot take anything away from it, you cannot add anything to it, it takes the place of any discourse and is sufficient unto itself.

14

The inner experience *

It was around that time that I began to glimpse one of those essential truths the search for which occupies us, at least intermittently, throughout a whole lifetime. My relationship with the world was gradually transformed by it.

Implicitly, my upbringing had taught me that there were higher pleasures and lower ones, that certain pleasures elevated the mind, while others debased it. Without things being openly expressed, it appeared that those which came within the realm of sight and hearing were noble – into this category fell the contemplation of works of art and landscapes, or the pleasure one took in listening to classical music – while taste, smell and touch offered only joys of an inferior sort (with a preference, nevertheless, for smell which one had to admit brought some elevated joys). Thus the pleasure taken in a good meal was insignificant, somewhat degrading, at any rate tainted with vulgarity – a pleasure of the body – while the sight of a banquet

---

* *'The inner experience of eroticism demands from the subject a sensitiveness to the anguish at the heart of the taboo no less great than the desire which leads him to infringe it.* This is *religious* sensibility, and it always links desire closely with terror, intense pleasure and anguish.' Georges Bataille, *Eroticism*, Calder & Boyars, 1962. The italics are in the text.

immortalised by the painter of a Roman fresco delighted one, quite rightly, since it involved a pleasure of the mind connected, what's more, with classical culture. Sexuality was not spoken about, though, in my opinion, it fell into the second category of pleasures, with the added weight of fear and disapproval that is associated with things so serious that they require silence. This set of judgments which permeated daily life, though never expressed, implied that the body and the mind (or the soul depending on the case) were two distinct entities, one inferior, the other superior, and that there was no communication between them.

I had, of course, like everyone, challenged the simplistic views of my upbringing, but my rejection remained intellectual, as I had not had a profound experience to teach me, *from the inside*, what a powerful link existed between the physical and the spiritual. And now, quite late in life, here I was discovering that a sensation, a simple sensation, like the weight of Julien's hand on mine, could be the key to the universe, the starting point to an experience without limits. Sexuality opened up a route that took one beyond one's usual state.

I now found profane vocabulary inadequate. I had entered another order of reality. To account for the distance separating the two worlds in which I now moved – that of everyday life and that to which I had access through love – I resorted to the notion of the sacred, or 'sacred eroticism', eroticism being in my view an experience of a religious nature, if one was prepared not to take the word religious in its narrow sense, when it is connected to a specific religion. This thought enabled me, in times of suffering, to dissociate entirely life 'in love' from life outside it: the two lives had nothing in common; thus I could accept, before I understood the need for it, the alternation between periods of inner death imposed sometimes by Julien's long silences, and the hours of extreme passion that followed, abrupt changes thanks to which we maintained the high temperature at which we lived.

The desire to place ourselves within 'a life in love' and escape stupefying routine made us refuse to be rooted in the quotidian. It would be more accurate to say that Julien refused, since, for a long time, while noting the beneficial effect of absence on love, and how much it increased my need for him, I had trouble accepting that which was causing me so much pain.

During the years that our affair lasted, our meetings remained infrequent, as I think I've said – frequent enough that we never grew accustomed to absence, far enough apart to make me long, often to the point of anguish, to see him again, to touch him. Every meeting was suffused with expectation that increased desire, and we never knew the misfortune of approaching each other with indifference. To what extent was the spacing of our meetings jointly planned? Constant travel justified it in part. But I felt rather that Julien was acting by instinct – true, instinct sharpened by experience – preserving both a freedom that was his very breath, and the novelty of a love that escaped habit. I never managed to distinguish in him how much was intoxication, and how much was composure and a taste for playing games. Composure prompted him to leave again and his taste for games to exploit such a tendency.

And I, impelled by a possessiveness that I could not overcome, even though I judged it severely, tried desperately to secure his love, to grasp that which eluded me. I might as well have tried to halt the movement of life. He had the gift of living in the moment, of throwing himself into it headlong, consuming life with an extravagance that never ceased to surprise me. Like a miser, I hoarded impressions, returning to them in moments of solitude, appeased only when I had managed to take full possession of them, as when, as a child, I liked to watch the circles produced by a stone on the surface of the water spread, fade, then disappear. The mirror of the water, as smooth as if the stone had never existed or been thrown, fascinated me because of the absence of any ripple, because of the restored calm that had engulfed the event.

This need for the extreme also made us reject explanation, clarification, reproach and recrimination, analysis of our differences and ordinary psychology – an exploration of the periphery that would have taken us far from the burning centre which was where we wanted to keep our love. Of course, this approach, which suited my taste for silence and his desire for harmony, did not bring only advantages; it involved saying nothing about too many things that were important, as testified by the brief warnings I sometimes found in Julien's letters – his freedom was threatened – or by my vague impulses to escape, to withdraw into myself, and my inner exhaustion. And yet – and I cannot emphasise this point too much – for a long time, these tensions suited what we expected of love.

15

*'And in voluptuous pleasures,
I languish with desire'*

Going back to my trip to London and the early days of our love, I don't think I ever spent so much time daydreaming in parks, only outwardly idle. Away from Julien, I could think about myself and gauge the strength his love gave me, reflect on the changes it had wrought in me; I had all the leisure to examine its effects.

It is pointless to dwell on the metamorphosis that all lovers are familiar with. Once, as a child spending the holidays with friends, I was struck by the sudden and truly astonishing change that came over a young woman's face within the space of a few minutes; dinner was interrupted by a telephone call and, silent as usual, she left the table to answer it. When she returned a little while later, she was like an apparition: she was literally radiant with happiness; she didn't say a word, no more concerned to tell us the reason for such a change than to hide the obvious signs of a state that placed her far from us, but her distant look, her softened features, her absent air spoke enough of the joy that filled her and was sufficient unto itself.

If love naturally increases the flow of life, what happens

when it touches someone in middle age – someone, like me, who had long felt paralysed, for whom the acts of talking and listening involved no real commitment, since they corresponded to a series of parts played by turns for the requirements of life in society, someone, though, whose profound immobility weighed her down, to the point where it felt like a kind of death? If one listened with one's heart, and not with the ear which catches only speech, to those who lack words or the talent to capture attention, one would detect in their apparent silence a call, a cry of distress, for their inability to translate the secret life within is equalled only by their desire to do so and, in the face of such a violent desire, they feel that all their efforts, all their attempts, like so many bottles thrown into the sea, are vain, destined to fail, always inadequate.

Thus, I felt unconnected to everything and, watching others as they moved about, it seemed that they enjoyed the happy contact with things denied me because of some strange flaw in my make-up, that they partook of a life that I was excluded from and this life I saw a little like a place from which I was barred because I didn't have a key. In fact, it was I who was locked in – shut up inside myself, unable to express myself, trapped by desires with no outlet (one knew one desired something, but what?) and roles in which I only half-believed, clinging despite myself to the promise of a more profound life glimpsed since childhood. But, and this was the question, how to reach this current of life that one can continually sense, when one doesn't have the means (and the means are numerous, writing being only one of the ways of attaining these living depths), when dreary daily routine keeps one in a sluggish state, separated, as in the punishment of Tantalus, from the things that one sees, unable to grab hold of them? One had to find the key to that other world. In other words, one had to find the way – for a writer, the voice, the small inner voice – that was one's own.

I do not doubt that this desire so long held in check, this long-hampered need to live constituted the main impulse of my love. It flourished because of the years of sterility, of ill-accepted immobility. In it were resolved the wanderings, the frustrations, the anguish accumulated over a lifetime. When Julien was inside me, I felt that I had lived only for that moment, that it justified the lost time, the vain desire, the suffering of the past, and the hours of malaise; and now not only could I see the reason for all that suffering, but it seemed necessary since the force of my passion stemmed from it. Like a patch of bright colour in a painting that balances masses and tones, giving them depth as well as a *raison d'être*, my love gave meaning to what until then had none: my past life arranged itself around him, or rather, everything in that life led to him. Would I have loved in that way, with the feeling that my entire being was opening out, if I had had an outlet before then, if I had found other ways of connecting with life?

From the day I loved Julien, things stopped being external to me. Life flowed in, torrential happiness. At the same time, my feeling of being invisible disappeared and, depending on circumstances or my state of mind, this sometimes suited me, sometimes overwhelmed me: I had become aware of my body – with the kind of awareness that draws the looks of others, since appearances are only striking because of the spirit that drives them. Because Julien loved my body, I felt it to be desirable and I was proud of it. Such a revival has nothing to do with youth; as a young woman, I had sometimes experienced a narcissistic pleasure in being looked at: I felt beautiful; but today I felt alive, and, since I owed that life to him, it was a gift far more precious than the beauty that was also restored to me. Like the young woman suffused with light who once made her appearance in the dining room as we were having dinner, I knew that I too was attracting looks due to the intensity of the feeling I carried inside me. It was at that time, I think, that, entering a restaurant one day while I was still full of our hours devoted to pleasure, I realised from the expressions of the diners at other tables that they *knew*: they read on my face the movements of the previous scene as clearly as if they had been there; there was in their insistent stares, I thought, more than the indifferent curiosity with which one greets every new arrival to distract one from the semi-boredom of a protracted dinner for two; a sort of surprise and, who knows, brief fascination; but, if this overflowing of my private life, this sudden disappearance of barriers, felt like a form of immodesty – had I not just opened the door to the white room and given them a glimpse of what took place inside? – I was not embarrassed by it, however, since to my mind it was natural that the rest of life should arrange itself around love. And is it not indeed strange that in everyday life more often than not sex is so perfectly covered up that there is nothing in one's behaviour or expression to conjure up the fundamental reality of desire (though advertising images play on it almost exclusively). The thousand attitudes of life in society endeavour to make one forget that which, nevertheless, counts for the most: the act of love towards which the day leads, later to be concealed by the night and the secrecy of walls? Everything takes place as if one is deliberately ignoring, in all the social relations that develop or break up from day to day, the possibility of a more precise connection, of a secretly desired outcome. One of Julien's principal merits in my view was precisely that, having made love his essential preoccupation, he never ceased to proclaim it, and with all his being: with his look that distinguished you from others, with his movements, with his laugh, his head slightly thrown back, with the expression of his mouth – both eager and weary – with the gestures that, though perfectly natural, since they followed the course of his changing moods, soon revealed the seducer – not the sort who, in order to please, resorts to techniques tested a hundred times, served up again at every opportunity: this was true seduction, its endless improvisations based on a real understanding of sex. Unlike those whose shyness condemns them to furtive, foolish boldness and who, one fine day, for instance, touch your leg under the table without warning, he approached love head-on, quickly declaring his intentions, not by some ill-timed gesture, but quite naturally, expressing the thought that was so intimately part of him.

Thus preoccupied with these observations, I returned to Paris. Not only had the uneasiness of our last meeting in public disappeared, but with distance and reflection I was filled with gratitude towards the man to whom I owed these discoveries. This was our first time apart. His voice on the telephone had the caressing intonation that always had such a powerful effect on me: hearing him, I already felt I was near him, merged with him, taken over, filled. The sound of his voice uttering the most ordinary words of tenderness, 'my darling', which he did often, the mere sound of that voice, when I had ceased to catch the meaning of the words, acted upon me like a spell, transporting me to another state, another world.

Before meeting him, as always, and even more so this time if that were possible, I got ready with a meticulousness, an attention, a care that was almost painful, so concerned was I to please him. However much he told me that, although it was my appearance which had attracted him at first, it was subsequently for myself that he loved me, I only felt calm – but how could I speak of calm when I was on my way to meet him with my heart beating as if it would burst, anxious to satisfy him this time as much as the last, anxious that the scene of seduction that occurred inevitably should commence – I only felt a little calmed when the mirror – mirror, mirror on the wall that never lies – reflected to my demanding eyes a presentable image, free of lines, dark shadows, furrows and other gifts bestowed by time. Rested, bathed, waxed, pumiced and perfumed, my nails filed and my face made up and powdered, I felt ready at last. My preparations had in fact begun the day before, for they required a long night's sleep; in truth, they were continual; no other major concern was to burden a life that I now intended to devote to love. In a last fastidious gesture, I removed a little of the surplus make-up, the excess powder that would have thickened my features and given me the artificial look that he did not care for. And what of the perfume that I had chosen after lengthy hesitation? It had to have the natural scent of flowers without its blandness or heady side, to be both gentle, sweet and subtle like jasmine on warm evenings that made one nostalgic for love, it had to be discreet yet easily recognisable, persistent without being vulgar . . . In short, I expected it to grant me the complex means of attraction that I wished to employ, to contribute to the magic of moments with which it would remain associated, perhaps to provoke in Julien – because, one day, in my absence, he would think that he had smelled it – an enhanced need to see me again. Had he not asked me, before we parted for a few days, to leave him the scarf I was wearing, an item of clothing impregnated with my scent that would stand in for me? It is likely that of all these roles the perfume chosen merely gave me a little confidence; I wore it only on these occasions and the bottle was added to the collection of ordinary objects used for our meetings, which love elevated to the status of sacred objects. I kept it for years, long after I left Julien; of the perfume there remained only a brownish, fragrant sediment.

When I didn't take the métro, which was rare, as I have said, as I felt that the descent underground, and then the ascent, suited the kind of journey I was making, I went to meet him by taxi. The trip gave me the chance to experiment on the driver with the effects of my recent efforts. This was not an attempted seduction, a second-rate rehearsal before the scene that was to follow, but I had noticed that love, either because we are looking ahead to it and the happy tension can be read on our faces, or because we are still bearing its trace, attracted without fail the attention of the men who approach us; I never aroused taxi drivers' interest as much as I did at that time, to the extent that during those first months one might have thought that, by some inexplicable coincidence, I had come across a different type of driver, more alert, more familiar, given to making jokes about sex, apt to be ribald if not forward. One day, one of them suggested that we stop at one of the sleazy hotels in the district we were driving through, describing in simple, precise terms the pleasures that awaited us there. I pictured the narrow staircase with its worn carpet as, one after the other, we climbed its steps, then the room with its big battered bed and bedspread of brown plush, unless it was rayon, soiled and shiny with the grease of use, and in a corner, the inevitable chipped and yellowed washbasin; I pictured the way that fat, ugly man would remove his clothes, his obscene nakedness and my lack of desire and, still picturing it, I considered the obscure fascination that revulsion can exert, the appeal it can have. If the driver was to be believed, quite a few women gave in to temptation and went upstairs with him in some shady hotel or other, spending an hour between errands, he had a number of addresses of such cheap hotels, he told me, it was his life, his real reason for living, and thus, before going to join Julien, I had met someone else whose life was, without anyone knowing, devoted to sex. These confidences and rather sordid images, induced by my state of mind and the highly amorous climate in which I was living, created a sensual turmoil in me. Desire is less delicate than love and it is stirred by the situations most opposed by the mind that animates them; I was tempted to see, if not a similarity between the taxi driver's offer and the promise of the white room where I met Julien, then at least a distant kinship, a common origin in what some like to call 'the mystery of Eros'; occurring at that precise moment, all of this brief conversation, which I would not even have countenanced a few months before, so distasteful would the notion have seemed, confirmed that, thanks to Julien, I had unravelled this mystery, that I could fearlessly accept, that day and the days that followed, to represent love, to maintain for him the state of a life in love.

I remember that when I got out of the taxi I left behind a book I had brought for Julien; the driver called after me, handed me the book and remarked before driving off: 'Admit it, I've upset you . . .' Of this adventure, which I recounted to Julien, hoping to surprise him and, perhaps upset him too, this was the only detail that he picked out, no doubt because he found the subtlety of this last pleasure alone worthy of interest.

Armed with the self-assurance that a glance or a word had thus given me, I rang at his door with a beating heart.

This time, the bell had only just sounded when the door opened slightly. Enough for me to be pressed against him a moment later, held so tightly that I was almost smothered, as if to stifle any distance between our bodies, wrapped in his arms, the only place in the world where I felt I belonged. It was his embrace, his warmth, his voice, his vivacity and his tenderness, his love of life and his profound anxiety, it was all of him as I had dreamed him a thousand times when waiting to see him again, as I had desired him a thousand times; during the brief moment I spent pressed against him, all of this was restored to me and I wished for nothing other than what was given to me: to look at him, hear him, feel him, touch him.

This meeting is part of the sequence, interspersed with breaks, of moments devoid of heaviness that Julien caused me to experience. By what unknown means, I wondered, did he bring me such a great, such an exquisite variety of sensations? Under Julien's fingers, I discovered that my body concealed an infinite range of possibilities. While he was caressing me, I observed myself all the time, surprised that a light pressure from his hand, a light touch of his fingers could have such an effect on me. When he was touching me, it seemed as if there existed a mysterious accord between our two bodies, a kind of intuitive understanding, imparting to his hand the required gentleness and firmness, granting it the precision required by the place he had just stroked. The skill of his movements – a skill that seemed inspired by the most secret desires of my own body – never ceased to be surprising in its refinement and accuracy. How, indeed, could he 'know' so exactly that that particular caress, at this point upon my body, which had become sensitive in its entirety, was the one above all others that I was yearning for, the one that would cause me a pleasure so acute that it was painful? A pleasure that is exquisite, to give the word the ambiguity it has in English where it is linked with pain as much as with pleasure, since it immediately produced a need for even more intense pleasure, an exacerbation that was only assuaged when, sometimes, in a paroxysm of excitement, he slapped me hard on the face.

I recoiled the first time Julien spoke to me of the need, at moments of intensity during love, to exert, or endure, violence. I recalled the erotic engravings and illustrations that I had found rather comical because, in their similarity and clumsiness, they revealed such a poverty of invention, having been succeeded nowadays by comic strips, more crude and more daring but devoid of the old-fashioned charm that was at work in the case of the former. It was the sameness, the laughable side of the theatre of perversion that Julien's words evoked. I responded by declaring my visceral and resolute horror of all physical violence. Briefly, summoned by my naïve fear, a vision of the feverish exhausted faces that distinguished the decadent era – Aubrey Beardsley's, long and bony, or that of Swinburne, a dwarf with a disproportionately large head – had crossed my mind, superimposed on Julien's features.

But the violence into which he was to initiate me – in a sense ritualised – a violence that was perfectly contained and measured, was quite unlike the pathetic gesticulations that the word had brought to mind. With him, I came to understand the need for excess that is linked to the ever greater exasperation of desire, the need to suffer or to make suffer, to subjugate or to submit, a need mingled with death, unfathomable and dark, which at its extreme leads to the need to kill or to die. But neither one of us sought the intensity of pleasure for its own sake. In my view, the slaps that Julien gave me resembled the symbolic gestures by which, in the theatre, as in the liturgy, one signified a sentiment, or state of mind: ritual, virtually impersonal gestures, whose meaning mattered more than their effect, in this case the aggression present in sex and the age-old dominance of men over women.

And it was indeed this meaning that he communicated

to me, when I was yielding to the desire to submit to his law, to surrender to it, to be annihilated, to cease to exist. This desire for abdication, which I accepted in love, when I was yearning for Julien to strike me or kneeling before him, how shocking I would have found it had I suspected it in any other situation, had I been tempted by it in my social or professional life, I who had based my independence and any success I might have had, on a refusal ever to be dominated, ever to give up a fraction of my duties or my rights.

Sometimes we allowed ourselves to get carried very far, as on the winter's evening when I joined Julien later than usual, in a room that the encroaching darkness was gradually transforming; in a far corner, we had switched on a lamp whose cone of light partially illuminated us, casting large shadows across the room. A deep silence contributed to cutting us off from the world outside, the very silence of the retreat of winter, when windows are closed, through which the sounds of daily life escape with the return of summer. Was it the new strangeness of this setting, the silence enveloping our movements, or the vision of an unknown face that the meagre light illuminated only in parts, singling out, as Julien moved, now his eye, now his nose, now such-and-such a part of his body, thus replacing a familiar being with another who was both close and unknown? I could no longer connect what was happening to any of my usual reference points. That night, I let myself drift off into pleasure, no longer concerned with union, paying attention only to sensations that were so acute that each one seemed to plunge me into an abyss where I lost consciousness. First, he made me lie down before him and, choosing to half-undress me, unveiled in turn, in the sparse light falling upon the bed, those parts of my body that had been covered. Carefully, gently, he lifted up my skirt – knowing his tastes, I had chosen a wide one – he pushed back the delicate underwear beneath it, then, with the same pensive gentleness, bending my knees, he spread my legs wide apart. He laid out my clothes with care, so as to emphasise the nudity he was uncovering. Having thus prepared me for a ceremony whose outcome still remained a mystery to me, he moved away, leaving me alone, exposed as if on a stage, spread-eagled; then, not taking his eyes off me, he went to his desk and listened to a letter he had dictated that afternoon. And by thus bringing together the activities of love and those of everyday life, devaluing the former by linking them to the latter, he gave new power to the feeling of being unveiled, exhibited – a power derived from the surprise and outrage. I was offered up to his gaze, just like an object considered by a possible buyer, in a position whose immodesty I felt, while from a distance, to all appearances indifferent to the sight, contemptuous even, though he had not taken his eyes off it, he contin- ued to conduct his everyday affairs. Then he came back over to me, still in silence; kneeling at the foot of the bed, he buried his face in the flesh that he had uncovered a few moments earlier, as if to pay homage to it having first abased it; and in this to'ing and fro'ing of love between low and high, in a debasement that increased the distance to cover, the source of the deepest pleasure became apparent. Lying before him, still half-dressed, I was, in his hands, something he could do with as he wished, as he turned me over and again back, kneading and massaging, engaged in a strange labour whose stages I was no longer following, occupied as I was only with registering the nuances of a pleasure provided by what felt like an extraordinary variety of instruments, at work on those points, the most intimate of my body – from the finest, the sharpest, the most penetrating, to the heaviest, the smoothest and the gentlest, and I did not know what was coming, going, entering, leaving, I could not distinguish between the precision of the caresses that came one after another and that of the blows that stung me at times, so pierced was I by the pleasure of both. I was now lying on my stomach on the bed, my hips slightly raised by a cushion, offered up; he had made sure to keep my face turned towards him so that he could watch the effects of climax on it. We were now a single tension, a single hunger to be merged. This fulfilment, this time he did not want, choosing to fight desire.

Now, standing in the darkness and wearing his coat, he looked as if he were about to leave, when with a rapid movement, as if to show me the violence of the control that he was exerting over himself, parting the panels of the coat, he undressed; at the same time, as if swept along by his movement, I slid to his feet and, kneeling there, gazed at his member for a moment: that point of his body through which surged such a powerful charge of life; then, with devotion, I took it in my mouth and, along all its length, felt its smoothness and power. Was it the night that hid our faces and erased our identities, isolating the part of the body observed and giving it a mysterious new presence, like the hard member of idols whose face is roughly carved, almost ignored? Was it the state of extreme excitement in which our abstinence left me? I had never felt to such an extent the respect combined with dread that sacred things inspire, or the desire to serve them and to prostrate myself. But he had wanted the last caress only to cut it short, and soon, pushing me away gently, he had the strength to pull himself up and move away; and again I submitted to this demand, knowing that if we had apparently ignored the essential, about which I could not suppress a feeling of revolt, I had also progressed in the science of pleasure, glimpsed the depths it could open up. Indeed it was simply a matter of increasing pleasure through deprivation, as I think I've said, and not of the asceticism practised by certain religions, an asceticism from which I understood only later how love could profit. The aim of transcendence did not guide our search, but who knows whether, matters of love not being clearly defined, this deprivation, to which I had to consent, did not benefit emotion? While yielding to the illusion of strangeness, I had not for a moment forgotten that it was Julien who was giving me such pleasure, he who was leading me into this unknown giddiness where the mind was well and truly forgotten to the benefit of the senses, and I would have obeyed blindly, whatever he had asked then, because it was he who was ordering me to do it and I wished for only one thing: precisely to obey him, to submit to him, erase myself, follow him as far as he wanted to go, even down a path that I would once have considered that of depravity – a word I will be careful not to use. And no doubt, at that moment, I wanted him to urge me to follow him down that path, for he had awakened in me an endless appetite for sensual pleasure, an inexhaustible greed for new caresses and pain, and I had reached that degree of submission that requires humiliation – a form of surpassing oneself, but from below.

He telephoned me the following day, troubled by our experience of the night before, troubled, he said, that he had forgotten me along the way, had let himself be controlled by sex, had lost sight of the 'flight' that we both expected of love. I understood that he refused the reversal which had tempted me, as he refused to venture further into those extreme states where ecstasy, linked to the exacerbation of desire – to go further still – meets the desire for death. But as I maintained that, even in pleasure, I had not for a second forgotten that I was with him, that it was him touching me, him taking me so far, he expressed a gratitude I had not expected: the power of such a love impressed him, he was moved by it and – I was even more struck by this wish – he hoped he deserved it, hoped he was worthy of it, and this, reminding me of the different levels at which we were each experiencing this passion, only inflamed me more.

Sentiment, taboo subject

*I am aware that in using the word 'love', or the word 'suffering',
one is breaking the tacit rules laid down by the contemporary
era, and one also exposes oneself to the risk of ridicule ('the
obscenity would cease if we were to say mockingly, "luv"').
Such a risk, as that incurred when resorting to language that
is unfashionable, should not trouble us: 'I take for myself the
scorn lavished on any kind of pathos: formerly, in the name
of reason, today in the name of "modernity", which acknow-
ledges a subject, provided it be "generalised" ("True popular
music, the music of the masses, plebeian music, is open to all
the impulses of* group subjectives, *no longer to the solitary
subjectivity, the highfalutin' sentimental subjectivity of the
isolated subject". Daniel Charles,* Musique et Oubli*).'*

    *Things have not changed since Barthes made these observ-
ations, or rather they have, they have got worse. A few decades
on, sentimental obscenity has lost none of its force, quite the
contrary. We dare approach the sentimental, but only indirectly, by means of a trace — material, if possible — left in
daily life. Nothing can exceed the unseemliness of a subject
who collapses in tears because his other behaves distantly, when
'there are so many more important things', notably the state*

of the world and 'all the horrors committed every day'. In the effort that society makes to refuse the idea of transgression, sex, once the taboo subject par excellence, has alone captured our attention, while sentiment has become the new forbidden subject. 'Love is obscene precisely in that it puts the sentimental in place of the sexual.'

But this is not my intention. It is not a question of swapping the two words, but of keeping them together, of reinforcing the significance that sex and love derive from each other.

16

The figure of the triangle

A few weeks after my return from London, we had the opportunity to spend several days together. A long July weekend had emptied Paris of some of its inhabitants. Despite his family's departure, Julien had decided to stay. I myself was there to meet a Swedish friend. We would thus be able – it would be the first time – to go for walks freely, like tourists, and, experiencing both pleasures and feelings of unfamiliarity, to rediscover landscapes to which the absence of Parisians and arrival of strangers, strolling idly, peacefully, along the banks of the Seine, would lend a mild, holiday air.

At the agreed hour, we arrived at the hotel where Liv, an old friend who visited every year, was waiting for us. I had said nothing to her about Julien, not being by nature given to confidences, and respecting moreover his desire to keep our affair secret. Only slightly younger than me, she had the bright face and smile, the translucent skin characteristic of people from Scandinavian countries. Julien noticed it of course, and I saw with satisfaction how attentively he greeted her; the day was starting under the best auspices. Needless to say, my pleasure at seeing my friend again, whose beauty I appreciated as much as her tact and discretion, qualities that would, I thought, be an invaluable help, faded before the excitement contained in this new situation: there were three of us, countless occasions would arise to assure myself of the complicity that makes a couple the most impenetrable of secret societies.

Unfortunately, it rained without stopping that day. We wandered the streets around the Odéon in a miserable search for a film that would interest all three of us. Evidently, we failed to find one. That left the cafés, neon lights and false intimacy of the banquettes. There was no way of finding any privacy, or having the conversations I had dreamt of, my friend's presence prevented it. The enthusiasm of the first few hours, those of expectation and discovery, was followed by a little weariness: the invigorating current that should, according to my plans, have passed between the three of us was not getting through. I must add that this friend, whose subtlety I liked when I was alone with her, retained in this very different situation the same reserve, the same gentle indecisiveness, the same taste for half-tones and unfinished sentences; she uttered cautious opinions in a muffled voice; in short, that day I found her singularly lacking in the vitality that gives emphasis to the slightest word and whose absence deprives even the most fascinating speech of interest. Our words gushed forth and remained hanging for a moment before landing and sinking into the neutrality that was insidiously gaining ground. There were a few exchanges, apparently trivial but that sent a shiver of pleasure in complicity; conversation, like a fire that won't get going, crackled and went out.

Amongst other things, we mentioned daily life and its burden of obligations, Liv looked so rested, how did she do it? Whereupon she described her exercise classes, intensive, rhythmic training in time to fast music: 'You're exhausted afterwards, but it does you so much good,' she added in her slack voice and I, who was feeling weak at the mere thought of such exercise – besides, hearing it described in that way did not make it especially appealing – remarked only: 'I'm permanently tired, so I can't imagine shaking in time to music only to make myself even more exhausted.' At that moment, Julien spoke up with authority, taking the side of the opposing camp that shook in time to music and whose merits I had sought to diminish: 'But that's just it, maybe you wouldn't be so tired if you did this kind of exercise.'

Nothing in these remarks departed from the strictly banal, and yet I liked feeling that I had been put in my place, and therefore laid claim to. Did the ease with which Julien dictated my conduct not imply: this woman is mine, and with his peremptory piece of advice, which treated my abilities and wishes lightly, was he not, indirectly, asserting something like a right of ownership? This was no more than a fleeting pleasure and almost an indication of what our conversation might have been, of what we were losing.

The hours stretched out and the talk flagged; sprinkled

with *double entendres*, whose somewhat forced use must at times have seemed strange to a third party, it did not succeed in reviving an intimacy that the atmosphere, as dull as the rain-filled sky, had loosened. Also, far from bringing me the pleasure I had expected, the day was unravelling, only just saved from disappointment by brief bursts of goodwill. A strange thing happened, moreover, breaking the bubble of safety protecting me.

We sat down in one of the brasseries opposite the Louvre, relieved that dinner would at last give us something to do. Under the harsh light of the ceiling lamp – the least flattering lighting there is, in which one easily acquires a cadaverous appearance – Liv still looked fresh and beautiful. The tension of the afternoon, which she had obviously not felt to the same extent, had left me feeling tired and I was aware of not looking my best. But nothing had yet come to threaten my happy certainty that I was alone with Julien, set apart from a world peopled with extras. This world – external, distant, devoid of real existence – the friend that I had brought, out of faithfulness to a long-standing commitment, she too belonged to it. But now, detaching herself from this backdrop, imperceptibly, she had come to join us in our intimacy, without my noticing how or when the move occurred: it was no longer just the two of us, we were now three. Julien's gaze, that I met just as often, far from expressing the exclusive awareness of my presence that I had found there earlier, was now moving freely from one to the other without making any distinction. He had left our universe and seemed quite untroubled by it. The conversation too flowed easily and, as we broached a historical subject that I knew little about and that meant a lot to both of them, soon it was unfolding away from me, without me. I felt excluded, exiled, gripped by a painful feeling of unreality, the situation had the gratuitousness and lack of an exit of a bad dream; Julien talked with animation, his body inclined towards Liv, and I watched, bewildered, the look of almost painful intensity that drew his features taut as he tried to convince her – I, whom no conversation in the world could have distracted from thoughts of him. But he seemed to have forgotten me, not even thinking, now, of including me in the dialogue, even if only with a glance, apparently fully absorbed by the subject he was discussing with Liv. I was near him and he didn't know it, at least that's how it seemed. The change had been too sudden, its effect was too brutal for me even to try to face up to it and to react; I sat there, motionless, paralysed, plunged in an uneasiness that was growing with every passing minute. At last, seeing no end to the nightmare other than through escape or, perhaps, through a gesture of generosity in which I tried to gather my scattered wits, I left the table once we had finished eating, and went to pay the bill. Often, in situations where I felt misunderstood, denied in my very being, I tried to re-establish my hold and a form of superiority by displaying a little haughtiness, an attitude which I must say, in my defence, was still a genuine attempt to overcome feelings judged petty or destructive and to recover, as well as a certain notion of elegance, the more flattering image with which I identified – a means of defending myself against the attacks of the outside world, of returning to a centre that, while not invulnerable, was fixed, away from the gaze of the other, a private, secret place: oneself, or one's image of oneself. My calculation proved to be right, as we shall see.

Julien and Liv left the table and came to join me. After dropping my friend off at her hotel, we sat in silence for a while, separated by a thick unease that I could not as yet decode, express. In the darkness of the car, I glimpsed his profile, the fold of his lips, his familiar tired, anxious expression, lit up by the light of the headlamps and, gradually, without a word of explanation being uttered, I let myself be won over again: the spell was at work once more. Drawing up at my door, he stopped the engine and, as we were about to part, he asked if I had enjoyed the day; I said no – just that one word: no. I had seen Julien give himself over to his feelings fully only on rare occasions; even in moments of outpouring, I sensed a secret distance in him; besides, why should his experience of our love be troubled when he was so sure of mine? But that night, as if that 'no' and the scene that had gone before had breached an invisible dam, he was mine without reservation, with a new abandon and wildness; even though he was holding me tightly against him, I did not need gestures or displays: I understood from the urgency in his voice, I saw in his distressed face, when he moved away from me for a moment, that passion gripped him at last, that it had risen to the same level as mine. Julien explained that, during the evening, he had not for a moment stopped addressing me, even when he was talking to my friend, that it was me he was thinking of all the time, not the subject he was discussing – in fact, the whole performance was intended for me – imagining furthermore the caresses that I could have been giving him, kneeling at his feet like the other night, hidden by the long tablecloth, and he no doubt enjoyed the deprivation as much as the images that it conjured. And he had appreciated my final gesture, which had given me the last word. Thus he was seducing two women at once, deceiving us both in order to stir up his desire and his love, but my love was not demanding when it came to the means used, or the honesty of the speech for the defence: it was enough to know that Julien loved me, and perhaps I admired him for being able to make the most of the situation, even by conduct that in any other I would have found trite, in order to increase the force of his passion. He loved everything about love, the game and duplicity amongst other things, however much he denied it; and, recognising in passing the tried-and-tested weapons of the seducer, I appreciated the flair and presence of mind with which he used them; in his case, rather than using them one should say he rediscovered them.

17

'Fulfilment'

After this, I could not part from him. The narrow space
inside the car was not enough. He took me for the first
time to the flat his family had vacated for a few days, to
the room he occupied night after night with his wife, and
I looked closely at every piece of furniture, every object,
every detail, because Julien had chosen them, they made
up the circle of his life, contained a little of his personality, of his tastes and preferences and, like his words, or
perhaps more so, since the overall effect was not planned,
they revealed what he was; for this reason, the backdrop
of his life, which I was seeing at last, was as precious to
me as his entire being. I will not attempt to describe the
moments that followed. The emotions of the preceding
hours together with the far more moving discovery of the
home in which Julien lived – usually without me, apart
from me, but this evening with me – these emotions raised
me to a level of happiness that cancelled out desire. I had
merged with him well before he entered me. That night,
he made love with a new intent, but I was occupied with
a single thought: it was *him* taking me, *him* in whom I was
disappearing, the anxiety on *his* face was the mark that *his*

love for *me* impressed on it. The act was less important than the idea: far from being a frenzy that seized us one dark night, I was aware this time of having transcended physical love, of being with Julien, by him, in him, without the need for sex, and this taking flight was not followed by the crushing collapse into a feeling of incompleteness.

However sweet the hours spent in Julien's daily surroundings, however soothing the movements that acquired a new familiarity on being inserted into ordinary life, I did not stay with him that night, and yet I could have done so. I wanted to spend a whole night with him as much as I feared it. He undoubtedly felt the same reluctance, for it was this diffidence that prevailed, this fear of a surrender of the self that was not the surrender of passion, consisting of a different kind of sharing, revealing the body in sleep, perhaps devoid of its seductiveness, the body engaged in its own movements and no longer driven by love. As we parted we made vague plans to spend the following night together, but the opportunity passed, neither one of us seized it. True, there were plenty of excuses for parting, his family might return a few hours earlier than planned, a friend who knew he was in Paris might catch sight of light in his windows and call in without warning, who knew what else? But the truth was, a shared night scared us. I link this reluctance to a phenomenon that might seem surprising and about which I have often wondered: my total lack of a wish for a life together; at no time, whether I was happy or unhappy, did I want to change the form of our relationship. From hours devoted to love to sharing our lives as the days went by, there was a huge step that my imagination was never tempted to take. Such was the force of my passion and its torment that it never occurred to me to link it to ordinary life. This at least was one suffering that I never had to endure. It is in the nature of certain feelings to stand apart from the everyday, with which they cannot be reconciled: they do not involve the qualities or moods that it requires. Convinced of this truth, I was grateful to my love precisely for taking me to the extreme states that I had obstinately sought for so long. A few hours once a week, before the far longer separations that he imposed on me, were enough, a few hours that had nothing to do with the rest of life, a few hours that required such a summoning of energy and were followed by such a state of absence that I could not imagine increasing them. As for Julien, this frequency suited his need for freedom.

And yet, how these everyday actions – a monotonous succession which I refused to share with him – moved me and filled me with joy when, the next day, he invited me to dinner at his home, and, had me sit facing him, in his kitchen, while he expertly prepared the meal. In fact, it was less a meal than a celebration. Every one of his movements seemed endowed with meaning, and that meaning was our love, and I watched the ceremony of preparation unfold, filled with gratitude, because the food he was preparing for us, as well as being intended for the body, was, through the joy that drove these actions, however ordinary, that of love. And for once I understood the Christians who had often been cited as examples in my youth, for whom no action was empty or pointless if performed thinking of God, for whom every meal taken in the light of that love came to resemble Communion, and the acts of everyday life, dull and repetitive, became charged with meaning. I had sensed this, though in a confused way, in my childhood when I was dragged to numerous religious celebrations, some actually very beautiful, with all the Catholic pomp on display, others more modest, in half-empty country churches, whose bareness, added to the officiants' clumsiness, may have highlighted even more effectively the symbolism of the attitudes. If I had always found the Christian concept of pleasure, which had to be repressed or sublimated, unacceptable, here now, sitting before Julien in an environment that admittedly lacked the solemnity of a church, surrounded by smells and smoke far more prosaic than that of incense, I understood at last the spiritual meaning of their celebration.

We spent time that evening looking at the vases made of semi-precious stone that he collected. He placed each one in turn on a shelf. We gazed at it in silence and, little by little, the harmony of its contours, the solidity of its shape combined with its translucency, the obvious fact of its presence, impressed itself upon us until it inhabited us. I *saw*. No longer the external forms, but what they concealed, each one of them: splendour. And this new way of seeing came to me from Julien, it was Julien who was giving me this power as a gift. Thus, having rediscovered the divine nature of the world, I was ready to enter into religion so as to worship at every moment him on whom it depended and who was its active centre.

The enjoyment that the shared meal had given me continued: Julien's presence was in me and his presence was sacred, was I not chosen, since such a thing was happening to me? I, for whom loving myself too much had never been a danger, here I now had the greatest respect for my body and my entire being.

That evening, after dropping me off at my flat, Julien telephoned. His voice, whose intonations I had not ceased to hear, like the accents of beloved music, resonated within me, and the words Julien pronounced were like an expression of my own feeling.

'Life can bring nothing more. I have now reached the most I can expect. You give me everything. I don't have a single need that you don't fulfil. There's nothing beyond that.'

I received these words without fully understanding them at first. At that time nothing could reach me any more, neither awareness of my happiness nor of what was being said, but I knew that I would endlessly return to those sentences: whatever happened in the future, nothing could take them away from me, nothing could make them unsaid.

18

The presence

Soon after, I went to the country alone. Julien could not
contact me there, but I didn't mind. No letter, no new
conversation, at a lower temperature than our last one,
would disturb the perfection of my present state. I would
return to the last few days and relive them at leisure, picture
again every one of his expressions, hear his voice, repeat
to myself every single word of the sentences he had uttered
and the ones I had said to him, not in order to seize from
his a new interpretation, as was often the case, or to imagine the effect mine had had on him, but to appropriate those
scenes and their charge of delights as I had not been able
to do at the time, stimulating my love by reliving the essential ceremony.

Those days were exquisite. I was free of the tension
that had filled me. Armed with a new confidence, I stopped
wondering about Julien's feelings and about the difference
between us – the state of obsession in which I lived, the
freedom that he had not relinquished. This was perhaps
the only time when I could believe that love had become
the centre of his life, that the whole of him sought it, without cease or rest, as I did, whereas loving was usually for

him like breathing, an action involving neither difficulty, nor anxiety, nor the kind of commitment that bound me to him, a commitment of the entire being.

For now, the certainty of being loved gave me peace and enabled me to enjoy, not without triumph, an unaccustomed freedom. The weather was warm and sunny, I remember, the grass was still high, and I spent hours lying in the sun, in the field in front of the house, doing nothing but staring at the perfect blue sky above, congratulating myself on my new vitality, fully experiencing the pleasure of existing.

The letter I found on my return to Paris was indication enough that I had not been wrong to suppose he was impatient; while all the sentences he wrote to me regularly seemed winged, conveying an impulse, a call, a desire that was undoubtedly addressed to me, but that in some way complemented the rest of his life, also consisting of impulses and desires, this letter, which was far longer, spoke of lack and need, exasperation at waiting, the single thought of love; it said 'my love': 'my love, how I miss you', and it repeated these two words, my love, as if in an incantation, it said 'I tremble', 'I tremble at the thought that you might leave without our seeing each other again', and it repeated the word, tremble: 'I tremble and I love you'. It said 'everywhere': 'I look for you everywhere; I mean that I miss you intensely everywhere, in every physical and emotional place in my life, Sunday, Monday, today' and it added three sentences about the word place, whose meaning, for many reasons, went straight to my heart: 'Any physical place is a psychological place. Any physico-psychological place is a possible point of love. Any place is a point of love for you these days.' And even if I wasn't too keen on that ugly-sounding 'physico' (but I had stopped being critical of Julien's letters), even if the indication of time laid down a restriction (but then no one loved the moment, the 'now' more than he), I felt that the letter was the expression of an exclusive, absolute love, sweeping all of him along, for the first time. There followed instructions, precise to the point of being meticulous (excessive precautions that I attributed to his anxiety), that would enable us to meet again before he left on a brief trip. The irresistible desire, the haste that propelled him towards me, the urgent need to be together, this too was what I loved in him. 'Quick, my love,' he said on the telephone one beautiful afternoon that I had decided to devote to work, 'Quick, my love', as I undressed before him. Quickly I went to him, gripped by mad joy after days of waiting. Life was starting again. But then, the impulse satisfied, he disappeared once more and time stopped, fixed at the moment of our last meeting, which I continued to relive.

The weeks that followed were calm, peaceful, devoid of excitement. An unusual feeling of fulfilment enabled me to progress in my own personal tasks with new pleasure. I wrote too, a vast number of notes in which I tried to free myself of the states of mind and various flurries of emotion with which I deemed it unwise to burden him.

Thus I did not leave him. The days passed. Filled with his presence, I did not wish to see him. From time to time, a letter from him arrived, a few lines, a sentence that matched my inner peace, as if echoing it: 'I'm happy that you exist.' Time suspended, unified by the thought of a single person, avoiding the painful multiplicity of my usual state: did I ever possess Julien as completely as during those weeks when nothing, not even he, came to distract me from his presence? And did I ever love him with such calm fervour? Gradually, I grew used to a deceptive tranquillity and to the idea that his love had reached the same intensity as mine.

'The task of the verbal signs will be to silence . . .'

Can we stop the plea that is inside us, even if it is unspoken (but it is rarely entirely so), from being sensed by the other? For that, we would have to be able to suppress it – in other words to suppress ourselves.

'. . . the signs of this passion run the risk of smothering the other. Then should I not, precisely because of my love, *hide from the other how much I love him? . . . I hesitate between tyranny and oblation . . . I am condemned to be a saint or a monster: unable to be the one, unwilling to be the other.'*

19

Subjection

By then, summer had arrived, and with it, the time for long holidays. We were both of us going on vacation (sinister word with its echoes of emptiness), by chance at the same time, though to different places. Julien had hired a villa in Italy with his family, while I was going to Greece as I did every year. I dreaded this first long separation, while he displayed a calmness that was perhaps not at all feigned. 'You don't lose someone because you're not seeing him for three weeks,' he said simply. Indeed. Also it was less the departure that worried me than his lack of anxiety about it. Here again, made demanding by success, I was seeking I don't know what assurance of his love, the expression of an anguish similar to mine, the certainty that he would miss me as much as I already missed him, a little jealousy of the friends with whom I was travelling, who knows? But at the moment of parting, on the doorstep, he said simply: 'Be happy.' This remark was like a viaticum during the long weeks of semi-solitude that I was to go through, this remark in which I saw affirmed not, as I should have done, a love of life and happiness, but a distance that hurt me, uttered without reproach or irony, with a slightly distant kindness maintained under all circumstances, I could not understand it, or rather, I could not accept it. And this time I resented him for a serenity that placed us so far from each other, when in fact it showed a confidence and generosity that he had made a principle for living.

It was in this unfortunately negative mood that I left for Greece. I had moved a long way from my fine demands, and for an apparently trivial, even derisory, reason; but I was conscious of nothing but the separation.

I was travelling with two friends. We would be crossing the Peloponnese by car, visiting the great archaeological sites en route, before choosing a beach in the south. The aridity of the landscape suited my mood. The brown, bare mountains, dotted, near Athens, with buildings under construction that looked abandoned, with their rusted iron needles rising up into the sky, in which I was tempted to see, rather than the result of a chronic lack of money, a tragic backdrop, an oft-used symbol of human endeavour and failure, of vain waiting and disappointment: the disappointment I had felt at the moment of departure which continued to act like a filter upon my way of seeing. During the entire journey, which I spent mostly in silence, without thought for my companions, words came back to me, memories, images, without my summoning them, soon covering, erasing new sensations and visions which too, infallibly, took me back to Julien, to scenes around which the entire being arranges itself, as a valley does around the river that cuts through it. It was not even that I was thinking of him: Julien never stopped being on my mind, an absent presence that 'distraction' hid only for a moment, returning it to you the moment after without your being able to do anything about it. Thus I often felt both the pleasure of loving and resentment at my captivity.

It was a strange trip, made in his tyrannical company, he who on the threshold of adventure had given me my freedom. Its great unity did not derive from the landscapes, which were broken up into a series of vignettes, or from the light on summer evenings that I love so much I return to gaze at it every year, or even from the negative mood that at first influenced the way I saw things, making me prefer the tragic to any other aspect of that country; it was made of relentless tension: I was directed towards Julien like an arrow aimed by an archer. And I saw things only in the hope of describing them to him, linking them to our love, writing for him fragments of the novel that I will never write. For I intended to captivate him as much with the resources of my conversation enriched with new images, as with the suntan and healthy glow acquired on the holiday; also, in order to remember them, I jotted down a few notes, as uninspired as they were well intentioned, building up a store of concrete details: he liked them. 'My room, with its bluish walls, looks out over the sea. At night gusts of wind make the ill-fitting shutters of the house bang. Every morning, the cracked, triumphant crowing of an old rooster awakens intermittent voices in the village. Then it's the turn of the donkey, and with him, we get in comic mode all the suffering of the world.' I noticed other signs of that suffering: 'Every morning, as we walk down the narrow street to the beach, she's there, sitting on her balcony, occupying its entire width: an old woman in black, hands lying forgotten in her lap, facing a model boat symbolising who knows what shipwreck.' Or a spectacle whose ritual side interested me: 'On the beach, an obese woman walks into the sea. Her ankles, strangely fragile, barely support the weight of her monstrous bulk. She sways at every step, escorted by a swarm of little children who grip and hold her up whenever she is in danger of collapsing, and her body with its unreal contours, an extravagant succession of waves of flesh, spreads out fantastically against the sky. When she returns to the shore, she lies down and drapes a white cloth over her face, then her companions gravely cover the enormous stranded form with sand, as if in a funeral rite. Perhaps her deformity, which places her outside the common run of people, has made her the equivalent of a goddess to them, a primitive Venus, an incarnation of fertility or a symbol of the eternal return, which dies and is reborn every morning.' But more than these gloomy sketches, which I made sure never to give him anyway, I liked the landscapes whose beauty gave me a feeling of limitlessness, as did my love sometimes. Blinding, absolute beauty, without nuances; present to the point of being a certainty, an answer to all the questions one would ever ask: doubt had no place there. It is; that is all, like fullness compared to our emptiness and, gazing at it, we leave behind division, anecdote, accident. Thus, the firm and irrefutable edges of the theatre of Epidaurus opening on to the entirety of the world for evermore, or the cypress-covered hills around the lonely ruins of Ithomi: they are preserved from life and from time, motionless, magically, in the duration of stone. Sometimes, before the spectacle of massive Doric columns standing against the immutable blue, I was struck as if by a statement by the hard simplicity of the line, the sharp contrast between stone and sky. Sometimes I was held by the mystery of a remote place occupied only by shattered columns, vegetation and the song of cicadas; then one expected to see the god Pan appear, hidden there for centuries, bearded and fearsome, whose subtle presence was revealed in these inhabited ruins. Sometimes, by the turquoise water's edge, lying on the sand of some deserted bay, I let the sun warm and soon burn me, until I experienced that all-powerful feeling that I sought, of being crushed, of dissolving. Such exposure to the sun is bad for one's health, one might object. Undoubtedly, but what did it matter, when I thought of the psychological well-being I drew from it. And always I came back to Julien: the thought of him never left me. Several times a day, I experienced to the point of pain the desire to see him again. The trip was in fact nothing but a long preparation for my return. At last, the day I had dreamed of a hundred times arrived. In the plane, I pictured the letter that would be waiting for me, and anxiety vied with impatience: what if, for some reason, I did not find a letter? An unbearable thought, a disappointment that I would not survive; all I could do for days, was to wait – or if his letter was calm, indifferent almost, as his farewell had seemed, what would I feel? I needed words on which my love could feed, words to appease its hunger.

I reached the landing, then the door to my flat, then the tray where the pile of letters lay, fear almost suffocating me; going through the letters that had accumulated over three weeks, my heart beating in my throat, my hands shaking. Amongst so many pieces of paper whose origin I didn't even consider, it was the Italian stamp that jumped out at me: out of a concern for clarity, Julien had written the address in block letters, so the handwriting was not recognisably his. The stamp blinded me – I can see it still, with the irregular stripes on the rest of the envelope. Tearing open this envelope, without my usual care, took no more than a second, but once the pages were before me, covered in characters whose shape alone overwhelmed me, I could not read them, my emotion prevented me. I scanned the letter, picking out a word here and there, no doubt to lessen the shock, giving a first impression time to settle in before I could face the letter as a whole, before allowing its full meaning to enter me. Thus I saw first the words isolated at the top of the first page, as if they were an epigraph: my love. It went on to describe the Italian light, his immersion in the landscape and the lack of birds, a surprising absence that Julien found disturbing – though in fact these details took on importance only due to the effect of those first words which endowed them with particular meaning, relating them to our love. I read: 'look for you', 'imagine you', 'bestowed upon me', before returning to the tenderness of the last lines of the letter, slightly breathless lines that ran, extended, stretched out and had no full stop, for they made sure not to conclude or specify, preferring to let my imagination construct and experience the sharing of which we were deprived, and the movements of love, and 'the thousand ways' for us to connect. The following day, a note told me that Julien had come home earlier than planned and was waiting for me.

It is difficult to recount moments of happiness when they assume a certain simplicity. This time, we were happy, simply, entirely. Julien undressed me hurriedly. When he saw me, he gave a cry (the memory, in which I acknowledge the part played by commonplace vanity, still today fills me with nostalgia), the new colour of my body, the even brown that I had so carefully worked at, transformed it, making it more beautiful; and I, I had felt rewarded for my efforts, proud of a tan in which he saw the effects of sea and wind, of hours spent in the sun, and of all my thoughts directed towards him, proud of the youth and beauty that I could still offer him, thanks to those weeks of summer. Over the years when I drew nude models at classes, I had noticed that bodies aged less quickly than faces; sometimes, a woman whose age could be read in her sagging features would reveal, upon removing her clothes, a miraculously young body, full gentle curves, touchingly beautiful. If I felt satisfaction when looking at my long and still slender body, I was harsh when it came to considering my face, which tiredness tended to weigh down. But that day I was young, and beautiful too, I was giving everything to him: our trivial conversation, our light-hearted mood, and the carefree moments that followed anguish and preceded new departures, moments free of heaviness, during which the mind takes flight, soars, flutters and looks down from on high, so that it seems nothing can reach it, not even that which usually frightens us, such as separation and absence which simply become episodes in a love that is invulnerable.

20

Tyranny or oblation

Julien was always leaving: London, New York, Berlin, summoned to one capital or other to appraise a painting. He was overloaded with work and worries, plagued by requests, exhausted, he couldn't see me. A fortnight passed . . . He sent me hurriedly written notes which traced his itinerary day by day, giving me lists of hotels and telephone numbers where I could contact him. One of these letters ended with the vision of a painting by Watteau that he had seen before he left: this time he did not say that he had looked at it 'trembling' because I was not with him, but rather, identifying with the subject depicted, he tried to restore some of the emotion caused by his presence, now denied me: 'Look carefully at the painting called *Muezzetin*,' he wrote, 'it's me (the very tender guitarist that you know . . .).' Indeed, I could see the aptness of the comparison, the combination of grace, tenderness and melancholy that he was laying claim to through the work of art (even though in his case the sadness was not caused by unrequited love, as was the Muezzetin's). But I was no less aware that I had been ousted from the image, that he had become its central character, while I was now no more than a spectator. Thus I continued to worry about Julien's failings instead of enjoying his gifts. And I wavered constantly between the joy that lifted me at the thought of seeing him again and the pain of knowing that I would have to return to my arid former life in order to find a little peace. In every word, in his letters as well as on the telephone, I watched out for the one that would assure me of his love – but nothing, no assurance, none of the 'I love yous' that he uttered in a light-hearted voice, was enough to appease my endless need of him, to diminish the constant feeling of insufficiency.

The difference between our ways of loving worried me constantly: in response to my demands minute by minute, to my thirst for him that nothing could satisfy, I got his evasions and reversals, his absences and returns; I did not see how love could be anything other than a total exclusive attention given to another being – an attention over which we have no more control than over the pain of toothache – and, in moments of weakness, I could not help concluding that if Julien did not love me in that way, then he did not love me. What was the meaning of the word love, and could one even speak of a sense, as if there was a single meaning, when such different nuances crept into it, irreconcilable requests, not to say insoluble contradictions, unbridgeable chasms? While confusedly aware that the peace of possession would have killed the passion, I suffered a thousand deaths in a situation from which all peace was absent. I would soon learn, silencing my anguish

– but did I ever stop suffering for all that? – to live inside *my* love without any longer measuring it against Julien's. Was not happiness being filled with his presence to the point that the need for his presence no longer troubled me? This happiness seemed to constitute a foretaste and promise of a more lasting state.

Twice only, I caught in his sentences something like a reflection of the tension in which I lived: on his return from London, where he had spent three days, I asked if he had thought of me, and he said: yes, he had thought about me constantly, to the point that his dread of an upcoming debate in public, which had gripped him as the plane was landing, had been a relief – the fear had been a distraction. But usually I did not dare beg for words of love, with which he was generous anyway, knowing that an assertion thus obtained was without value, and besides, powerless to mitigate my passion. My silence, I thought, would be a substitute for wisdom, for if I asked for nothing, if I managed to control the violence of the impulses that shook me, how then would he sense my impatience? Naïvely, I was satisfied not to let him even suspect what was going on inside me. And I promised myself that I would acquire the strength that enables one to experience happiness at what is given to us rather than to feel deprived of all that we lack.

Of course, an expression of my anxiety did not fail, without my being aware of it, to seep into my letters; and no doubt my expectations could be detected in many other ways, proof of which I obtained before long in the most distressing manner. And yet, a telephone call and the sound of his voice were all that was needed: the current flowed again, life returned, circulated, I was happy, enough to risk every boast and proudly declare: 'I have enough love in me to make up for all the insecurity in the world', a sentence he did not fail to notice with an admiration that may have been mixed with relief. And once I was with him again, there remained neither doubt, nor question, nor rebellion – nothing but joy, the feeling of coming alive again, a lightness of my being. The hours spent together, I told myself, had such power that they cancelled out everything else. 'What do I care what he experiences away from me, what he sees or what he feels, what do I care even whether he loves me at this very moment, since I no longer have any need. My love no longer depends on him. Nothing can undermine it.' And this independence, unthinkable a moment ago, compromised a second later, threw me into euphoria.

Indeed, he had only to withdraw a little of the attention I had grown accustomed to, for me to see how fragile such 'independence' actually was. Once again, there was the weight of suffering that removed my wish even to breathe, depriving me both of the ability to distinguish people and things, and the possibility of turning to them in an attempt to escape him.

'The circumscription of pleasures'

In Les Enfants du Paradis, *the most beautiful French film ever made, we see Garance and Baptiste in a little garret with the light of the full moon coming through the window. They find out that they love each other but, at the moment of embarking on their love, Baptiste runs away, making that love for ever impossible. Instead of the feeling that Garance offers him – 'Love is so simple' – he wants something else: a love like the one he feels: 'I would so like you to love me the way I love you.' Instead of accepting, he makes demands. This is the mistake that he tries, in vain, to correct in the second part of the film.*

A great deal of the literature devoted to love has looked at the insurmountable problem that Baptiste suffers from – that of simply accepting what is given to us and silencing our demands. If I could manage to confine myself to the lively pleasures the other affords me, without contaminating them, mortifying them by the anxiety that serves as their hinge? To take full advantage of them and place within a parenthesis of the unthinkable the periods of depression that separate them? Impossible, conclude the most pessimistic: 'I can certainly imagine procedures to obtain the circumscription of my pleasures (converting the scarcity of frequentation into the luxury of the relation, in the Epicurean fashion; or again, considering the other as lost, and henceforth enjoying, each time the other returns, the relief of a resurrection), but it is a waste of effort: the amorous glue is indissoluble; one must either submit or cut loose . . .'

21

Disreality

If one receives a telephone call every day, week after week, and then one day the call does not come . . . Who can describe the effect of such a break in habit, the state of near-madness into which it plunges us? And what of the habit of seeing each other, even if only for a short time, once a week, no more, less even, but reliable, a reliable habit, when the meetings become less and less frequent, to the point where there no longer is a habit, to the point where only absence and torment remain?

And then, charged with such a degree of hope, our meetings were not all equally successful. Sometimes, I struggled in a nightmarish unreality, without managing to connect with him. Like the day when, abandoning one of our usual rituals – the haste of our greeting – he led me calmly to the table where, I remember, reproductions of Rembrandt engravings were laid out, so as to describe to me in detail one of his recent discoveries. Whether it was this slight break in the organisation of the ceremony, the anxiety – always quick to flare up again – that suddenly crept over me, or his apparent calm, so out of keeping with my agitation, the fact is I found myself suddenly gripped by a sort of paralysis: I could no longer see Julien, no longer hear him; my own words rang false, my voice sounded alien to me, as if it were being imitated by someone outside me, I heard it but did not recognise it. I had entered an empty zone, a pocket of nothingness where all communication with Julien was forbidden to me; doubtlessly he was there right next to me, but I had no way of assuring myself of his true presence.

Seeing my distress and no doubt being subject to its contagion, he tried this time to help me recover my footing by pointing out a specific detail in which I would recognise him: the crimson of a bookbinding that he had chosen himself; for a few seconds, remembering our conversations on the subject, I felt hopeful again before night closed in once more upon my anguish. What followed was not the result of an impulse, but an attempt to escape an intolerable state, an expedient. I did not want to make love any more than Julien did; and yet I let him lead me to the bed, whose covers he had turned down in readiness for a very different moment and, despite myself, despite ourselves, the movements followed one after another. Performed from the outside, they somehow took hold of us, rushing us like an infallible machine towards an outcome that we had not wished for. Something had been triggered that was far stronger than my will and demanded to be satisfied, something that one could not provoke with impunity and to which I chose to entrust myself for the time being, to surrender all of myself to, to submit until I died (how I wished for death at these times), as one can choose to let oneself be swept away by a wave when one knows it is useless to struggle, that no human strength could resist. One moment, leaning over me, regaining control of the situation, he asked me when it was already too late, when I was already nothing but consent: 'Do you want to, do you want to now?' I had to emerge, however, from the oblivion into which I had slipped, from the absence that we had neither wanted nor prepared for; it was not followed by the state that usually succeeded it; barely had he let go of me than I was once more overcome by a feeling of loneliness and depression all the more awful as there was nothing to be done about it. He was near me, but I was alone, and how bitter is the loneliness and wrenching pain of being apart. For today, when we were forced vainly to re-establish contact, like those other times when, giving myself up to pleasure, I was asking him to fill a void as vast as my desire, sex had proved powerless to satisfy the demands of the mind from which it remained separate. Thus I saw with fatal clarity the error in wanting to appease my hunger for this man and his love with the brief illusion of fusion that sexual pleasure offers when it is limited to itself. Every time I tried to lose myself in orgasm so as to find peace, it left me more alone than before, and more bewildered. I noticed that it only deepened, exacerbated the feeling with which I had approached it: fury, isolation or despair. And yet I had no doubt that the body was innocent (an innocence that had struck me resoundingly when I had made love, not expecting anything other than pleasure, with men that I did not love or loved little), but my passion, in its absolute rigour, had led to these complications in which I was losing myself.

On the contrary, if the body and mind were one, if love inspired every one of my movements, if I approached it with full violence, then the awareness of loving culminated in pleasure that was not followed by a fall, but lasted for a long time in a state comparable to taking flight: far from pinning us to the ground, pleasure carried us to heights at which I strove to remain.

But I had reached a degree of passion where the intensity of the feeling was so great that happiness itself became confused with suffering, the inner turmoil so strong that peace became inconceivable. And all my reasoning, all my findings proved to carry little weight in the face of demands that I could no longer control.

I was afraid of overwhelming Julien with my devouring need of him and resolved, like the members of a religious community in their monastery whose example haunted me more than once, to resort to a discipline that would restore in me the order that love required. Besides, the failure of our last meeting had served as a warning: carnal love, for all that it was an entry into paradise, could also open up hell; I had to get some distance so as to prepare myself for it and approach it in the required frame of mind.

Desire of the absent being and desire of the present being

In fact 'isn't the object always *absent? – This isn't the same languor:* Pothos, *desire for the absent being, and* Himeros, *the more burning desire for the present being.'*

Thus the Greeks had already found a word for the ill that I was suffering from. Pothos was familiar to me. Himeros was the hunger that nothing, neither presence nor orgasm could appease. 'The object is there, really, but I continue to miss him, in my imagination.' (Barthes)

22

Stretching

It was at that time that I embarked on strange gymnastics of the soul, the idea for which had occurred to me while listening to certain pieces of music, particularly Beethoven's symphonies, which had a special power over me. Through the transcending of the self, in which all suffering is done away with, music, as the sight of Greek columns against the sky had once done, made me attain what I called inner unity, in other words emergence from the state of separation in which we usually live. Carried by the sounds, which undertook to express love, abandon, triumph or distress while removing all individual character from these feelings, I looked down from very high upon my love, also relieved of the personal aspect that weighed it down and made me suffer; how simple loving seemed, once doubts and questions, demands and anxiety and the need to be loved back had been put aside: I dreamed of a freed love in which neither egoism nor self-interest any longer played a part, of a truly celestial love, in the image of the music I was listening to. While the notes held me suspended, lifted as it were out of the sorrow from which they had pulled me, I gave myself up to a feeling of exultation; a miraculous accord, that seemed to be of a physiological nature, had developed between myself and the music: it resonated in my body as if issuing from every one of my cells; I was both the instrument and the composer, the symphony and the listener. Beethoven expressed the emotions that were troubling me and transcended them, rescuing them from their pettiness and restoring the breadth and nobility that was their essence. Thus, briefly, the music returned the breath that I had found in love. As soon as the notes fell silent, however, I was forced to fall back into my usual state – to be limited to myself again, without the succour of art, and the return to everyday heaviness made me feel exiled once more.

But what the piece of music had taught me was that, as Proust puts it, 'in all love, the general lies beside the particular'. I too would learn to move from one to the other, would practise the gymnastics that consist in living both at the heart of a situation and outside it, on two levels simultaneously, one personal, the other not. Rising above a feeling and its limited origin, it was possible to live, at least for a few moments, by observing it from afar despite the pain it caused, by looking down upon it, so that with distance it lost some of its power without, however, ceasing to exist.

No doubt love and the questions it continually raised were teaching me to understand better 'the substance of which we are made', but it also showed me how to leave myself in order to love more, love better. These discoveries filled me with gratitude towards Julien, to whom I owed them, towards the man who brought me this extra life: my love fed on pain as much as on joy, and on the work that the pain made me carry out on myself. I loved him partly because, for him, I had to put into play all the ability to love that I possessed, to give more fully so as to compensate for what he was not giving me. However, deep down inside me, there remained, intact, the desire to know, a watchful curiosity that owed nothing to love but was concerned only with making use of its discoveries, and this passion for knowing, I knew, would outlive the passion for loving.

Of the utility of loving

All I have to do is change the words in this sentence of Proust's,
replacing 'woman' with 'man' — which, in addition, has the
advantage of establishing the equality of the sexes in the face
of suffering in love — and I arrive at a conclusion that applies
to my situation and whose clear-sightedness pleases me as much
as its quiet boorishness:

'. . . a woman is of greater utility to our life if, instead of
being an element of happiness in it, she is an instrument of
suffering, and there is not a woman in the world the posses-
sion of whom is as precious as that of the truths which she
reveals to us by causing us to suffer.' (Proust, *The Fugitive*)

23

'I plunge and am engulfed'

Christmas came and, with it, more departures. I left for the mountains. More than any other stay in a snowy land, this one was like being buried. The snow fell, silent, slow, inexorable and, from my window, I watched it pile up, each light flake separating me a little more from the scene of my emotions. The snow was the only, the universal reality, and the turmoil of the last few weeks gradually subsided, covered like the landscape by the gentle whiteness that was not life. All that remained was an immense surprised peace and quiet in the bosom of which, now safe, though like a dreamer trying to pull herself together after the uncertain images of the night, I examined the agitation that had gone before, the feeling of insufficiency that followed our meetings, that exacerbation of the desire to love that nothing could now satisfy.

Considered against the limitless distances, deadened by the muffling snow, the turmoil died down. I had moved far, very far, into another region, a white abstract world, whose thick, hazy, indistinct borders were constantly retreating and extended everywhere, making any thought of escape impossible. Like the blanket of fog in Cocteau's film *La Belle et la Bête*, closing in around the unwary traveller, making him a prisoner of the enchanted kingdom for ever, the opaque horizon seemed less to mark the boundary between two universes of a different kind than to close off definitively any path of return to the previous state: there was nothing beyond this ghostly dreamlike world.

Everything seemed unreal – the figure of Julien receding until it was about to disappear, blurred by a mist in which contours melted, and the inner impulses that had, endlessly, like an obsession, supporting themselves, caused me so much suffering. In this state, as if anaesthetised, I could no longer feel the slightest emotion connecting me to him, nor even find the memory of an emotion, which would at least have been a sign of life. Deprived of feelings and of the very ability to feel, I was in fact separated from myself as much as from him.

English has short, powerful words to express such absence: dull, numb, dead. I remembered what a friend had said to me about love – about the choice one has (choice? only in a manner of speaking) between a dull, permanent pain, and violent, raging, unbearable toothache. She had forgotten, I thought, the condition of non-existence where nothing remains but a slight feeling of disorientation.

Nevertheless, for 9 January, in other words shortly after my return, I find in my diary only these words: my love. Powerlessness to describe the state into which I had been plunged by the fact of seeing Julien again? Surprise at the sudden flow of life that contact with his body had re-established? Exhaustion caused by the sudden move from one situation to its opposite? Evidently, I was short of words, too dazed by the violence of the emotion, by the sudden acceleration of life after the apathy of the preceding weeks to worry about describing this new miracle in detail. I saw him and nothing else mattered, neither past nor future nor thought nor desire, everything was cancelled out by his presence, by joy restored. Every time, the feeling of being reborn, of emerging from a tomb-like darkness into the radiance of life. As if that emergence had required an arduous solitary journey, an initiation process, preceding the rebirth, that involved a death-like state. I gave myself up unreservedly to this *volte-face*, the moment that followed could easily be the moment of my death – a few minutes ago I was still there – what did I care? In that very instant, everything was resolved, everything: pain, drought, waiting – nothing mattered any more, only this joy.

The feeling of liberation accompanying it explained our lightness, the spirit of playfulness that sometimes moved us, when we laughed at everything and nothing – at talk that made no sense, anecdotes of no interest, movements that had the innocence of those of the first people in paradise. The price to pay, however heavy, could not call into question this happiness, since it bore no relation to it, since it was, as I have already said, of a different kind: to evoke it, I could find only the words light, love, union, but used in their religious sense, when they imply an exaltation of

the entire being cast out of its usual c
ing another state. It was inside my absorpti
the moment when I had most entirely renounce
that I found my greatest freedom. Thus I lived from
crisis to another, torn between two modes of being,
between a search for purity that made me follow the
mystics' degrees of amorous ascension, and the exhausted
state in which my efforts left me, between selflessness and
the banality of possessive love, between a taste for pure
generosity and relapses into ordinary selfishness.

The interlude of sleep and distance had given my
passion a new impetus. Lying beside Julien, I looked at his
profile, the slightly heavy overhang of his lips, and felt as
if 'annihilated' by love – a gentle sensation for which the
mystics have found the term 'to be engulfed'. The kisses
I placed on his cheek, his eyes, his forehead, resting on
those parts of his body, came nonetheless from the soul,
for, as I kissed his face with devotion, what showed through
was – I had a precise image of it – our souls mingling.
How else to conceive of those hours during which, lying
naked side by side, we no longer knew either limits or
constraints but felt only our freedom – those hours of intimacy that followed love when, like the figures painted by
Tiepolo on the ceilings of Venetian churches – the chosen
ones rising and whirling, as if snatched up by the blue of
the sky – we found ourselves endowed with a kind of
weightlessness?

ndition and reach-
n in Julien, at
d myself,
one

frequent, once a week at best,
one. d one day that seeing each other
at that rate mean e were 'fully present' every time,
and I suspected that this 'presence' might be an effort for
him, the burden of love finally becoming unbearable to
the one who was the least in love, as I was later to confirm.
On the telephone, he described his tiredness, he was
exhausted, overburdened with commitments, he felt
broken, 'pulverised', 'stunned'; or else, to keep me patient,
he sent me frequent brief letters, the way he used to at the
beginning of our love, but their tone was quite different;
in the one dated Friday, 8 March, 'at dawn', as he speci-
fied, I read: 'My darling, I have been (am still) truly snowed
under this week'; what task required him? Who was harass-
ing him thus? Julien mentioned a mysterious 'they', and I
thought sadly of the 'they' in English nursery rhymes that
blamed all of society, the 'they' that, this week, removed
any possibility of meeting and therefore made him suffer
as much as me: 'This is just a bad patch . . .' Was I not
being invited to feel sorry for him, to help him by my
understanding when the world was conspiring to

overwhelm him, invited to stand by him, fraternally, forgetting my own desires, not demanding selfishly to see him, which only added to his burdens? Of course, I understood this implicit request, but I felt my patience deserved a concession, and this new delay annoyed me. Also, I took it very badly, the following week, when I did not receive his agreed telephone call, which I awaited with growing tension, and this time I gave in to a need for recrimination that seemed justified. And then, how could I accept, I who lived only for him, that my love, instead of helping him, instead of being a support to him, was a burden, an obligation added to all the others?

Julien was due to call me after a meeting to arrange a time for us to see one another the following day. The hours passed, the telephone remained silent, I was gradually overcome by anger: I was ready to imagine neglect, avoidance and I, who would usually in such a case have found ten interpretations favourable to our love, soon accepted only one, Julien had not kept his promise. It was then that I decided to write to him. It took me no more than a few minutes and, without giving it any more thought, impelled by the desire to relieve a little of my distress and, for once, to register my disappointment, fearing also that I would go back on this impulse a moment later, I posted the letter immediately. I asked him simply why he had forgotten to phone, I could not understand it. Some of my resentment must, however, have shown through, since it was to this hinted meaning that Julien responded, as if he had been waiting only for this obscure rebellion to express freely a weariness that had been building up for some time. He sent a few dry words by return of post: he had telephoned twice, as he was 'meant to' (and this 'meant to' hurt me), but it was before I got home, and after that he had not been able to continue phoning; he was 'at the end of his tether, swamped by a thousand exhausting tasks' (that he didn't describe), he needed 'lots of space' to find himself again; and he ended with a warning that sounded like an order of retreat: 'Help me by leaving me to it.' Today, I re-read this letter with indifference. At the time, I was shattered by it. In the chaos that it produced inside me, as one hangs on after a disaster to the swirling debris that remain afloat, I tried to seize scraps of an explanation for this un-accustomed brutality.

Fleetingly, I was tempted to link it to jealous suspicions I had recently felt, awakened by his recent air of absence, and by a name that recurred in our conversations. It was the name of a woman with whom he had been friends for years and whom I had come across a few times in literary circles; I admired her for her look of intelligence and the upright, strong, passionate personality she was said to have. His references were so slight that in all logic I could not draw any conclusions from them; I came, however, with-out further proof, to convince myself that he had rekindled an old affair, and to try to imagine this woman and the place she had in his life. In fact, it was an exercise I had already engaged in many times. But then, her image started to obsess me. I pictured her eyes, which were large and thoughtful, the charm of her smile, the air of sadness she had sometimes and, imagining that he loved her, I began to love her through him with a painful, captive love, full of fascination, adding to her slightly austere beauty the character traits that such looks would seem to reveal and that had bound Julien to this woman for years.

But another explanation caused me even more pain, so that was the one I adopted, suspecting that it was closer to the truth.

Our ideal relationship, crossed by neither complaint nor reproach since we each endeavoured to be what the other wanted, had half-hidden from me (but only half) precisely how much the effort was costing him. Not only was I discovering that my demands – so rarely expressed, so discreet, I thought (but can one hide the intensity of a love and the way in which one experiences it?) – were weighing him down and that he needed to distance himself from me, but I felt as if I had done something wrong, had failed our love by having claimed as a due that which never is. And, in an impulse more excessive than my earlier anger, wishing to make up for my rapaciousness with proof of abnegation, I decided not, as his letter suggested, to allow him a little freedom, but to 'give' him the space he was asking for, in other words to do what would cost me most dear in the world: to stay away from him, for good if need be. Despite the inner storm that was shaking me, I was well aware that this great leap was not without calculation on my part: by removing myself, I undoubtedly wanted to let him live his life, but I hoped above all to move him with my magnanimity, to make him fear losing me, and thus to increase his love. I was prepared to step aside, to disappear, giving up a need as vital as the need to breathe: that of seeing him. This approach only achieved its secret aim because I was fully prepared to take the consequences: without anything to ease it other than a very uncertain hope, I experienced the wrenching grief of breaking up with him and I was able to write him a letter, in response to his, that was undoubtedly sublime, absolutely sincere, that made me cry a great deal and relieved my sadness a little.

Strategy

Out of weariness or anger, we sometimes take heroic decisions — even a sham flight is one — whose secret purpose is to make the person we were pretending to keep away come running. We then play a game of loser takes all. Acting as if we were the underdog all the better to gain the upper hand. Or revealing dramatically a card kept hidden until then. Alerted by my hints that I'm leaving, the other will rush to hold me back. Meanwhile, he will have realised how much he misses me, how much he loves me. The problem in a game like this, is that the original stake is high: I can only convince my partner that my intentions are real if they are in fact real. Flight is a call for help: I flee from you so that you can pursue me. Even so, one needs to have reached the stage where such flight becomes necessary, in other words a state of weariness that can no longer be borne (one is still very far from definitive weariness, the kind that comes before a separation). And even then, there is no certainty that one will be believed. That is the risk of a game where the margin for manoeuvre is narrow. A game where one's entire being is at stake.

25

'Enthusiasm of virtue'

Often, in hours of great distress, I turned to writing, noting down my reactions throughout the day. So as to continue being connected to Julien, so as to make the pain of being away from him cease during that time, I wrote endless letters that I never sent because in them I described in their nakedness impulses that I would not for anything have let him see.

'The times when you demand the most from me are those when you expect nothing. If you expect nothing of me, I cease to exist. I have no explanation for this feeling; it's not an affinity, or even desire, you have taken possession of all that I am, in a profound, vital way that escapes reasoning. Why does one love someone? How to explain the "inscription" of a person on you? Of course there is no reason for the violence that is being done to you, no reason at all; this is how it is, it stems from nothing, from no particular feature: there is only one need that goes beyond us and binds us to the other, implacably. Sometimes we start loving that which did not attract us at first and we can no longer do without it. Someone has got inside us, becoming our inner law.'

Indeed. And why should this come as a surprise? One loves with one's entire body, the rebellion of the mind is only superficial.

While his letters had the impulsiveness of a cry, a few words written as they came to him, in a great disjointed surge, mine were long pondered over and often corresponded to my second impulse – that is, to the impulse I *wanted* to have – expressing not a voracity that would have frightened Julien, but a patience that would reassure him, not greed in savouring the slightest of his acts and moves, but gratitude for what he gave me. Writing a good love letter was no less satisfying than receiving one, and the feelings I described, being simpler and more generous than they really were, provided me with a model, uplifted my spirit, stimulated my love. Julien's letters were short, frequent and quick. Mine, calm and lofty in tone, resembled sermons; he thanked me effusively for, very fortunately, he was not given to irony.

The letter of parting, rewritten many times, refined until it attained the desired degree of calm and detachment, must have surprised him in its simplicity: I had removed from it any expression that was too narrowly selfish. 'The space that I have taken from you and that you demand back in your letter, I give it to you,' I wrote, and I had crossed out 'despite the wrench it causes me'; then I evoked the image of "The Waltz" with which everything had started; our love had remained faithful to that impulse and to the momentum it had conveyed to me. It was joy that gave me the courage to leave, I maintained in all sincerity, choosing simply to say nothing about everything else. I ended my letter on this positive note, on the happy devotion with which, for a year, I had kept Julien's presence in me. And it is true that beyond the feelings of doubt and revolt, the periods of drought and jealousy belonging to the dimension of the everyday, my love had not stopped growing in the other and clinging to joy.

And yet, as I wrote these noble pages of renunciation, crying from sadness as well as emotion at the beauty of my gesture, I had the feeling that I was posing. So, should I have given myself up to my inner agitation and poured out my disappointment in pages full of petty reproaches? But, once more, I found my best defence in an attitude that satisfied me morally, aesthetically. If I did, in the end, 'behave well', was it not to triumph over myself and him, as much as out of true magnanimity and a concern for love? Whatever the complex origins of my decision, I paid a high price: in posting the letter, I felt I was signing my death warrant.

Winning

In the game of love, what preoccupied me most, still, was winning. Or, more exactly, proving to be superior to the circumstances. Of course, this secret desire to win, hardly conscious in fact, did not in the least contradict my desire to lose myself in the intensity of love. 'Love is wanting perdition', a statement in my opinion more accurate than its opposite, 'Love is wanting possession'. But losing oneself is not losing, it is even quite the contrary. When we have tried in love to show the best of our self, when we have succeeded in presenting to the other an image to which we are attached, it isn't easy to lose the results of so much effort, for, as much as with the loved one, it is with all this arduous construction, which is inseparable from him, that we are in love, and this is what we do not want to relinquish. Self-love.

As for the letters, I quickly understood that, when one is writing to a lover, it is less out of a concern to reveal a truth than to make oneself be loved. 'You should therefore seek to tell him what pleases him most rather than what you think,' says Mme de Merteuil. But I did not need her advice in order to work this out. In the war of seduction, it is obvious that the roles can be reversed and that the conqueror must in his turn and for ever be conquered.

26

The hour of lead

I spent the following days in a state of exhaustion that took the edge off my suffering. A poem by Emily Dickinson came back to me. I found some solace in repeating it to myself: 'This is the Hour of Lead,' she wrote, and I felt that 'hour of lead' bearing down on me with its full weight. 'After great pain, a formal feeling comes – / The Nerves sit ceremonious, like Tombs – ' After sorrow, there is indeed a sort of peace similar to a state of lethargy, as I experienced then: this extremity seemed like a place where nothing could touch you any more, where you were indifferent to what usually hurt you. I felt out of reach there, withdrawn into the deepest part of myself, in an inaccessible hollow. As if respite had come after entire days when the very act of breathing was painful. Emily Dickinson calls stupor the convalescence that follows suffering: a state of apathy in which one no longer asks anything of oneself, one is happy simply to feel nothing – no more than that. 'A Quartz contentment, like a stone – '

But at night I would wake suddenly, pierced by a sharp pain, I thought I had lost Julien and did not want to go on living. I had had vague urges to leave before; true, they had only consisted of a respect for his own silence: I had neither called him nor written; but, on hearing his voice again, after days of non-life that had left me isolated in a distant world, subterranean and closed, I had not a vestige of strength left to resist the impulse that was pushing me towards him. This sound that I was hearing again, the sound of his voice talking to me when I thought I had lost it, was, with the cessation of pain, a surge of life so powerful that I could hardly bear it. I was hearing his voice, that was all, his voice. And I swore to myself that in future, whatever he did, whatever he said, the mere joy of his uninterrupted presence in me would be enough. By my own fault, I had seriously jeopardised that presence, without which I could not live. And yet, could I, this time, have saved myself a gesture of generosity and the semi-calculation that it concealed? I concluded that I could not and thus sometimes blamed myself, sometimes absolved myself, returning endlessly to our letters, to the shock that his had been – the sudden sense of being crushed – and to the momentum that had swept me along while I was writing mine. And prevailing over all of this, the feeling of loss. Of course, I scribbled a number of letters that were not at all peaceful and that I did not send him: 'I have done my mourning (so, at least, I thought). You can't imagine how unhappy I have been before reaching this stage, not knowing where I was any more, crying everywhere, in the métro, at home, at work . . . This feeling of dying, and wrenching pain, experienced physically – and waking with a start every night, night after night, as if I were being stabbed, with the sensation that I no longer had you, that I had lost you . . .' and so on, my silent complaints continued.

27

Turnaround

Several days passed in this state of mind before the letter arrived that I had been waiting for with all my being. Julien was writing to me, so that meant that we weren't separated, perhaps he was rejecting my suggestion, perhaps he wanted to see me again. But already this sign that he had not disappeared for ever, that reality had not closed up over his absence – had it done so it would have ceased to interest me – brought me back to life. I guessed that it would be his handwriting on the swollen envelope before even seeing it.

If I had always found it difficult to open his letters, so shaken was I by anxiety, one can imagine how I trembled with fear this time. As when I returned from Greece, but for opposite reasons, I found it impossible at first to read it. As long as I did not know its contents, the letter I clasped to me, bearing my name and the date stamp, a letter from *him* to *me*, attested that we were bound together, that nothing had changed. I clung to a hope of life. Then, unable to stand it any longer and without even intending to, I tore open the envelope impulsively and read the first page, not understanding it at first; my general impression was that he was thanking me, the rest seemed enigmatic: 'Thank you for your immensely kind letter,' I took in. 'In it, I found in all its breadth who you are, which is so dear to me. I've received it, but I'll need time to gauge all its implications . . .' The sentences that followed did not enlighten me: they revolved around Julien's mysterious state and his inability to answer me. What was I to conclude from this? What did the time that he was requesting mean? Would it end in him accepting that I had left him, or was it nothing but a hidden refusal to consider this possibility and my suggestion, as his last lines implied? In short, I felt that Julien was avoiding the issue once again by not facing up to my disquiet. But that may, after all, have been wisdom on his part: he was continuing along the path that we had settled on at the start, the refusal to engage in analysis or futile discussions. The end of his letter – an answer to the question that I had not asked – resonated like the most beautiful, the most reassuring of affirmations: '. . . I can say: yes, you're very present in me, I love you.' But there followed no suggestion to see each other again: we remained no less apart.

I did not hear from him again for a fortnight, during which time, instead of delighting in that 'I love you', I continued to wonder about its meaning. Thus, many times, out of a lack of trust, out of an impossible need to be appeased, I wasted the happiness that Julien was offering me. And I did so despite my resolution, putting aside my petty anxieties, to take only joy.

Then I received another letter, a longer one this time, posted in Brittany where he had gone for a rest. In it he described the landscape, and this landscape resembled him: it was all breaks, successive planes, 'sea against rock, rock against sea', and the backdrop had become the excuse for an attempt at explaining his deepest nature; 'nothing explodes, everything resolves itself into transparency and foams in the light, rocks become crystal . . .', and these tremendous collisions of sea against rock, though they might at every moment have conveyed the image of a final explosion and the idea of death, ended in ethereal, iridescent effects, weightlessness of the foam gushing forth into the light . . . Similarly, his life felt like a series of 'vertiginous' shifts, of 'truly painful' gaps, of 'abyssal' experiences that gave rise to a leap not towards death, but out of the prison of the self, towards the loss of self; afterwards, he concluded, 'one picks up the pieces and the process is truly creative'. The turn of mind as well as the vocabulary of the letter were fundamentally romantic, something Julien hid as best he could with a modern, prosaic expression – 'picking up the pieces' – that revealed the work of creation to which he attached the greatest importance. I could not help finding excessive his display of familiarity with depths, and I therefore suspected him of complacency. And then, with what calm egocentrism did he talk about himself, describing his states of mind and forgetting mine, on which admittedly I had laid little stress.

Yet I was moved by his attempt to analyse himself, when

he was usually reluctant to do so. Not that it told me anything new: I had, I think, a fairly accurate idea of the image he had of himself. But I understood that he wanted to have me know him as profoundly as possible. And, what counted even more, the last lines linked me to the revelation he had had in that rugged landscape: at the moment when he had reached an essential truth about himself, when he was conversant with notions of life and death, it was me that Julien had thought of, it was me he was with, it was by me that he had wanted to be understood. 'My darling, I can say this,' he wrote at the end. 'I thought about you there. I can say this: I was inside you there.' This direct reference to our intimacy caused the desired turnaround. In an instant I went from despondency to joy: those few words literally lifted me from the ground; in a flash the world had changed. In the euphoria that seized me, I did not resist the desire to call him: no sooner had I put down the letter than I was dialling his number. He was there, he was waiting for me. A quarter of an hour later, the time it took me to jump into a taxi, I was in his arms.

But that day no tenderness came to lessen the violence with which I returned to him. A little of the resentment that I had felt must have remained, combined with a deeper fury at not being able to stop feeling the separation and disappear into him in this embrace, for ever: it hardly mattered to me just then whether I loved him or hated him, connected with him or confronted him. I gave him nothing, not an ounce of myself, but only satisfied my most burning desire, experiencing to the very end what I had to experience. Not for a second did the thought of what he was feeling concern me, nor the need to share: I sought pleasure and the oblivion it brings only to escape the continual suffering of my tension towards this man. And we made love this time with a sort of rage, like a will to erase, to destroy, the other or oneself, what did it matter? In both cases, does it not involve ceasing to exist? Death freed of the dying. Thus I hoped, quite mistakenly, to appease in pleasure my need of him, or perhaps simply to forget him. But the hours and days that followed my exasperation at this meeting were dry and empty; brought back down to earth, left to myself, I felt nothing but loss and lack.

28

Anxiety

Not long after this scene, my negative mood changed. We must have exhausted a little of the rage that had thrown us towards each other, for I find in the rough drafts of my letters dating from this time lines of a quite different tone. Incapable of expressing the force of my passion, I made use, as in some prayers of invocation, of repetition, to write a letter to Julien's invisible double with whom, without fear of overwhelming him, I regularly discussed our love at length. This letter, like many others like it, was never sent.

Sometimes, I managed to maintain my state of elation for a few days, then gradually it faded, and an oppressing need overcame me once more. Sometimes, only sadness followed our meetings; I found myself back out in the street after a last embrace, as powerless, as bewildered as if he had thrown me out. And, adding to my dismay, the reason for my feeling abandoned escaped me; it seemed the gates of heaven had, without explanation, closed behind me, and the grace of loving that had lit me up just beforehand had – but for what transgression? – suddenly been withdrawn. The desolation of these moments that took me from the closed door to the entrance of the métro, when the momentum of love had deserted me like the fading effects of a love-potion, and a feeling of emptiness and deprivation replaced the euphoria of the previous minutes . . . I made my way back down the long corridors in a state of bleak despair, knowing that only another meeting, which might not take place for some time, would cure my growing dissatisfaction. It isn't so much that I need to see him, I thought, what I can't endure is the feeling of being apart. Because I feel the separation throughout my body, like a weight that is so heavy it crushes me, pushing me into the ground with every step, and I can't live any more, can't breathe, can't think when I don't see him. If I manage to love him enough that he lives in me without the deceptive succour of his presence, then this doubt and need will come to an end . . . But while I waited for this difficult transition, sometimes I foolishly resented him for his inability to give me what my love demanded, sometimes I thanked him and loved him like a god because his love required so much of me. Sometimes the discrepancy appeared, irreparable, between reality and my longings (and I berated him in insulting letters that luckily I never sent), at other times the gap was filled, he was once more the one who transfigured the world and, like a breath of air on coming out of prison, joy restored made me light-headed.

'You're nothing but an excuse enabling me to make what I have in me come to life,' I wrote to him amongst other polite remarks (letter not sent). 'A mannequin lacking the right proportions, too small for the clothes that I intend for it.' If I quote these lines today, it is because of the shame they inspire in me. For it was obvious I who lacked the 'right proportions'.

No doubt I soon realised that the love of a person was also, and perhaps above all, the means of access to something else – to a state of unity of which I had had an intuition in childhood and had sought constantly from then on; it was like an escape of the self, leaving the here to return to an elsewhere for which it had remained nostalgic, I thought, recalling philosophical works read long ago, whose accuracy I was now verifying in my own body. But could I hold it against Julien that he was not always the magic link between two worlds that were so far apart? And, if I did not succeed in crossing the boundary between the two, or if the spell did not last beyond the event, should I hold him responsible for my inadequacy? Should I demand that he give me, through carnal love, which had quickly become a drug, the means of taking flight whose effects I had so rapidly exhausted? Whereas, in his wisdom, he avoided the too-frequent meetings that caused one to fall into laxity and routine.

In this regard, however, we understood each other without need of explanations, for we were profoundly similar.

One day, in a conversation that was merely concerned with other people, I must have let show some impatience and a wish to be reassured, since it was to this wish rather than my words that Julien responded. I had said to him:

'The boredom that one can experience in a group, or

even alone with another person, is, I find, due to a feeling of limitation. I've thought about it, it stems from coming up against the limits of others, as well as one's own for that matter. But, from time to time, we meet people with whom we breathe more easily, more freely (he liked the word breathe so I used it constantly). Facing them we have the feeling that they have resolved or gone beyond the questions we are always tripping over, while with others, we sense they haven't even asked themselves the questions.'

When mentioning these people, in the plural, I was thinking of him, of course, of Julien, who to me was the lifting of the limitations that in others I found oppressive, him, the only being with whom obstacles and frontiers disappeared – not because of some knowledge, that seemed very ancient and had always surprised me, but because I loved him. But I said nothing of this to him, no doubt wanting to arouse his curiosity and prompt him to question me. And I added, I think, some banal comment about the feeling of isolation one often suffers from in a group.

'Living is like being above a void,' he answered. 'Nothing is ever enough. One finds only compensations.'

This statement of unaccustomed solemnity, made with a sombre distant air, was certainly not intended to comfort me: love was neither the centre nor the justification of his life – which was what it had become to me – it was nothing but a 'compensation'; it too in the end was not enough, a brief flowering of the self against a background of nothingness. Despite the sadness that it caused me – for, that day, joy had deserted us – I felt an immediate solidarity, I understood him: I always understood him.

We both aspired to the limitlessness of love. We both went through periods of drought when, lacking love, we suddenly gauged the extent of our poverty. It was the need for transcendence that united us, as well as the deep anxiety that lay beneath it. However, though so alike when it came to the essential, we were also very different. Faithful to the masculine principle that destined him for action, Julien sought the limitless through quantity and lined up his conquests. As for me, the calling I now followed, having fled from him, it is true, was to allow myself to be absorbed then and there. Thus we embodied the opposite and complementary natures, usually combined in each person, of man and woman, and, though we marvelled at our similarity, we prepared, according to the law of the misunderstanding between the sexes, to move further and further apart. For a long time I had marvelled at how well suited we were to each other, a miracle that occurred time and time again, to which contributed even those aspects of our personalities that seemed to work against it. Then our differences became more marked – but these differences too had seemed destined to stimulate love.

Undoubtedly, from the very first day, Julien's feminine side, consisting of charm, gentleness and apparent fragility, had struck me; he was continually in danger of being captivated by any force, and I liked this vulnerability. But instead of yielding to this force, he was crushed by it unless he sought in his turn to subdue and make use of it. And I liked this utterly masculine side too (I loved the combination in him of a constantly receptive sensibility and a subtle power to dominate that which impressed him). He was therefore not devoid of feminine traits, just as I was not without masculine characteristics. But, on the whole, few men exemplified as well as him the male instinct, few women as well as me the feminine, he who sought to renew himself in the indefinitely repeated actions of love, I who wished for only one thing: to dissolve, disappear, lose myself in him. Nothing inspired me with as much fear as dispersal and surface agitation, incessant eddies that drag us far from the still centre where life becomes perceptible; I needed to go down deep into myself, far inside, as if to an underwater cave, and retake possession of the treasures of the moment. While he never lingered in a sensation, impelled by his need for novelty, driven to start again, to live intensely, to throw himself headlong into new love affairs, new experiences. And he crossed on the surface the distance that I made my way through in the depths, so that the gap between us grew all the time, even though we were always pursuing the same goal.

Drawing on my reading – Plato, or Yeats perhaps, a poet whose spiritual approach interested me – I tried to describe this discovery of a fundamental difference in general terms, as if it were a law, distinguishing between two sorts of people (by which I meant of course him and me): 'Those who retain a yearning for the original unity try with all their being to return to it, seeking to gather within them, in a state of fusion, the scattered elements with which they are never satisfied in isolation. Others try to capture the totality, not in a single act of union, but by their adherence to multiplicity, in an infinite fragmentation of their being.' I was rather pleased with this little passage, as the idea of fragmentation, which had recently occurred to him in regard to himself, might convince him of the soundness of my thinking and make him forgive what he would undoubtedly be tempted to judge as pedantic abstraction (he had often warned me against my tendency to theorise). But he made no comment. And anyway, if I hoped to bring our two approaches closer together – in other words, to make him faithful, like me, for all these lofty thoughts boiled down to this simple calculation – was the attempt not doomed to failure in advance? Was it not deluded to want to change him? However much I impressed him with the depth of my love and the cultural models it followed, it was not, I knew, by such means that I would obtain the total reciprocity of which I dreamed, even if they did secure me his gratitude, his respect, a certain pride . . . And yet, I had not given up on trying to make Julien more in love with me, in other words on making his attachment an exact replica of my own, a perfect coincidence of feelings that to me signified a state of permanent bliss, an absence of the reversals that were killing me, and, above all, an assurance that love had become, as it had for me, the success of his life. This last point indeed tormented me most especially: without such certainty, I felt that I would never find peace.

Inflatable doll

The reproach of inadequacy. Uttered by those who feel they are not loved enough. No doubt the loved one is inadequate, but only when faced with outrageous demands. As if the other should transform himself and assume the size required by our desire, to grow fatter or taller, to bulk up a little here and grow a little thinner there, to swell prodigiously or shrink depending on circumstances, all of it so as to conform to our idea of the right size (right, in other words the one that suits me). 'The other owes me what I need.'

One must know that the love one has for another person gives us no rights over him. Whoever claims otherwise is dangerous.

29

Seduction

During this entire time, if what Julien later claimed was
to be believed, just before we separated, he was not really
being unfaithful to me, at least as he understood it: a few
flings no doubt, a few incursions without future, out of
curiosity, the need to seduce and be seduced, a few old
mistresses met up with again and honoured, not without
emotion, a few affectionate habits of no consequence, but
no woman came anywhere even remotely near, he assured
me, the central place that I occupied. He found the question bizarre, irksome, pointless, and he looked vague when
he answered, as if he were trying to remember. It went
against his theories about freedom and the idea, defended
time and time again, that 'you don't love someone any less
because you love others'. Equivocal as always about the
word love. As for me, his answer enabled me to discount
once and for all, at the moment when it became pointless,
a doubt that had long been torturing me. Even so, I still
had the satisfaction of knowing. But had I received an
answer to my question at the time when it was troubling
me, the semi-certainty would probably have made no
difference: had he not striven to maintain my doubt,

carefully keeping his secret, giving me information – like clues along the way in the kind of game I loathed as a child – only to complicate it immediately, out of the blue providing me with the precision that he had refused me the day before, or filling in his timetable, by confessing to some innocent occupation, such as a visit to a museum, a space that he had left blank and that had appeared to conceal a formidable threat? Sometimes he returned from a trip and told me on the phone that he was busy, that we'd see each other the following day, or in a couple of days. And I was in despair at the thought that something or, worse still, someone might be keeping him from me. Sometimes, with an absent look in his eyes, he seemed to be gazing at a vision that was denied to me and that I imagined, because it remained inaccessible, to be beautiful, profound and very seductive. The unknown unfurling behind his dreamy expression, the mystery of his life and his being – this was what I was in love with. For, in a way, was the distance into which he stared, beyond me, not a reflection of the elsewhere that I so wished to reach, where I hoped vainly to join him? Reasonable arguments that tried to relate the origin of his absences to specific, limited incidents, counted little: my love, beyond any likely cause, showed me the essential need of his nature, a need for the limitless to which I always responded.

I now believe that, like all true seducers, he was fully conscious of employing an amorous strategy, which moreover rather suited his desire for freedom, measuring out the advances and retreats, the gift of his presence and sorrow of his absence, doses of confession and doses of silence, making use of his taste for escape and the dissatisfaction that came naturally to him and so intrigued women. But I wouldn't want it to be thought that this was a matter of cold calculation: Julien had a genius for improvisation, if he allowed himself to be guided in his discoveries by his long-proven skill in love. Also I had guessed his ploys, but in my eyes his sincerity always prevailed over his game-playing; sometimes, during a conversation, I could see that he was lost in a memory, enraptured still, or troubled and exhausted, happy or despondent depending on the day; so I too felt joyful or weary, as if we were driven by a single spirit, as if we were one: he no doubt let me see him in all his inner variations in order to stimulate my love and my jealousy — for the mood that had come over us was combined, I felt (and he knew it), with the sadness of knowing that I was not its cause, that another woman perhaps had provoked it and continued to occupy his mind in my presence. It is no less true that he went through these states, experienced these feelings with the intensity that was characteristic of him. And I shared them. He made me suffer, as required by love that wants us 'to love only that which we do not possess entirely'; yet, because he truly loved me (even if his love did not resemble mine), he wanted to spare me suffering, a dual need that partly explained the contradictions in his behaviour and the swings that caused me to alternate between peaks and precipices.

He never spoke to me openly about the women who passed through his life; I was kept on the alert by comments of a general nature, on life, love, women; or else he mentioned a meeting, perhaps trivial, on which he did not dwell: on a trip to Lyon, he happened to have a conversation with the director of a museum, an intelligent woman, whose projects interested him. Another woman had come to visit him, a poet, incredibly neurotic, he added, but a real writer, aware of the importance of every letter in a word, who spoke perceptively about literature. Knowing that there was a chance of him finding any woman attractive, even if she was only moderately so, as long as she was sensitive and intelligent, my imagination exhausted itself trying to determine the qualities of which he had just given me a glimpse and that had attracted him, the specific affinities that would make this newcomer the next passion of his life. More difficult, and more painful still, was imagining qualities that were entirely different from my own and yet touched him, to the point where he might prefer them – imagining that he experienced pleasure with a person different from me in all respects, giving him sensations that I wasn't capable of giving him, that he was happy with someone whose nature and manner did not resemble mine at all, in a world in which I did not exist.

If I felt a sense of desecration at the thought of another

woman touching him, far greater was the pain of imagining a form of spiritual intimacy between them.

Intensified by his absent-minded air, my jealousy crystallised, for want of a more specific medium, around one of his women friends whom I happened to meet again at that time, at the private viewing of an exhibition. I had only to see her for my imagination to give form to a story that had so far remained in shadow. It was the woman with the pensive eyes whose presence had already troubled me. I spoke to her for the first time that day, prepared to be charmed myself, in all my emotion forgetting the paintings on the walls and the crowd around us, both wanting her to learn of my relationship with Julien – a link that connected her to me as well – and dreading it. She was beautiful; above all, she had a look of reserve and inwardness such as one rarely finds and which is like a sign of the soul in one's gaze (I had started using the word soul again since loving Julien; it was all the more appropriate here because this friend had a reputation for mysticism that would have been enough to isolate her from her circle and make her interesting to me). I felt fascinated by her instantly. Her image captivated me, and the emotion of our private conversation in the crowd remained linked with her, the moment when she spoke to me, to the exclusion of the people with her, as if she recognised a secret connection between us. As I fell in love with her face, Julien's faded from my memory: it was the woman's smile, her long eyelids, her fine skin stretched over the structure of her cheekbones that I recalled, and the distant air that Julien must have liked, and her tallness, and her elegant limbs. Starting from her features, every one of which I considered indicative of her character, I tried to imagine her life, her work, her thoughts and her attraction to God, in other words everything which, it seemed to me, fed her understanding with Julien. She came to obsess me, so that gradually the reality of the beloved's presence in me faded. I wondered whether she and Julien had made love and, unable to imagine that he had not been charmed by such a gifted and alluring woman, concluded that they must have; the rest followed: not for a moment did I imagine that she might not find Julien attractive. What change did pleasure imprint on her features, what became of that air of reserve and dignity when she abandoned herself to love? And if the gift for seduction is measured by the difficulty of the conquest – for I knew that Julien had a constant need to confirm his own – was it not more flattering to be the magician who caused such an upheaval than the humble artisan in his turn taking his place amongst many others? I pictured her head thrown back and the expression of her half-closed eyes as she let herself drift off into pleasure. Inevitably, an image came to my mind: that of Bernini's St Teresa, erotic and mystical, whose lips parted in an inaudible cry; her air of blissful agony was added from then on to the means of my torture. Knowing the nature of Julien's anguish and sensing the desire for the absolute that inspired his friend, I had an intuition of a love drawing on the deepest source, a love that bound them indissolubly. It resembled my love for Julien so closely that it was hard to tell them apart, in truth it was like its successful double, always being similar to the highest moments from which my painful imagination had worked. I loved that woman. I would have liked to observe the transformation of her face during pleasure and note the effect on her of Julien's power, a power that, by a strange aberration, became mine too. I wished passionately to share with her the novelty of our common discovery. And perhaps I loved Julien all the more for having been able to hold and enthral such a remarkable person. My suffering was mingled with a dubious pleasure. It was then I began to glimpse the strange phenomenon of identification with the lover that I would fully experience later on.

This obsession went the way of many others: it was based on nothing but vague impressions and faded by itself, to be replaced by some new, less troubling idea suggested by a word or expression of Julien's.

It wasn't so much jealousy that made me suffer. When all was said and done, I wondered little about the areas of his life that Julien kept hidden from me, since my imagination lacked elements on which to work. A different question occupied me – what was this love of which he assured me and never bothered to define? When I wrote him the following sentence, carefully slipped in amongst other more trivial ones, and whose sense he would grasp, I knew: 'The need to surpass myself is the very form of my love for you', why did he not answer in the same terms? Surely because his desire to surpass himself, though often expressed, was not concentrated in his love for me — because I was not the person amongst all others who would enable him to give form to such an aspiration. And indeed, it was all too obvious that his love required no effort, no tension, perfectly confident as he was at every moment of my love for him.

I tried therefore to imagine the woman who might have this fabulous power to attract Julien's entire being, body and soul, in other words to reach and possess that which had always escaped me. And inevitably, I fell into the trap that I was doing my best to avoid: possessiveness.

Jealousy

To act as a screen, this is the expression that best describes one of the strangest mechanisms of jealousy: someone comes between us and the loved one, putting him in the background. We feel growing love for the victor, less a rival than a successful double of ourselves, endowed with the qualities that have made her loved and which we do not possess, or possess to a lesser degree (since she is preferred to us). I therefore come to exaggerate the importance of that which I lack, in other words that which I admire in the other, and I stop loving myself, for want of reasons for doing so: my victorious double exists at my expense, feeding on my own substance, exists, while I, emptied of myself for her benefit, have well and truly ceased to exist. She has, in a way, become the luminous image of which I am now nothing but a negative.

How can we believe we are loved when we are thus made of dark, almost invisible areas, deprived of existence in fact? All one's work will consist in trying to 'get oneself back': in trying to love oneself, or, on the contrary, in sinking even deeper.

30

Chastity

I had noticed that after those meetings that were most highly charged with emotion, instead of success stimulating his desire to see me again, on the contrary it favoured Julien's silence, which sometimes lasted for days. As if such an expenditure of his being had rid him of desire, enabling him to recover and to distance himself. Having satisfied me, he felt liberated, absolved, available to the other lives that awaited him.

Learning from his example and convinced of the usefulness of a strategy, I resolved to make our meetings in the white room – those high-wire moments in which we both, without admitting it to ourselves, expected to achieve the same success – even less frequent. From now on, we would see each other only in public. I hoped that these meetings, where desire would be ignited but could not be satisfied, would recharge his love while easing the continual pressure of an exigency that I now knew he sometimes found stifling – had he not one day asked me to give him more space? The element of danger – for, wishing to spare his family, he made sure that our relationship did not become known – would be an additional stimulus, a minimal danger, admittedly, in a large city where the chances of being seen together were less likely. But I knew Julien had a taste for secrecy. The mystery of the parallel lives he led, revealing to each woman only a fragment of them, like so many layers around the central core that they protected. 'We're outlaws,' he said to me one day, not without pride, 'and we follow their rules.' This clandestine existence suited love, a secret ceremony celebrated as far away as possible from daily matters, and I had never wanted to question it. But now, feeling the need to 'air' our love, I was going to subject it to the test of a change of context, in other words of contact with the outside world.

When Julien phoned me, a long period of time, two weeks perhaps, had passed since our last meeting, and fervour had given way to impatience. I wanted to take advantage of the new momentum that our time apart had given our love. I announced that I would not go to meet him this time; I would rather we meet, for lunch, which would be a change, at La Coupole. I had carefully chosen the restaurant, which was full of people throughout the day, popular, at that time, particularly with writers and people in publishing, and where one often saw famous faces. Instead of expressing surprise or pique, he agreed immediately to my suggestion. The alacrity with which he greeted this novelty made me think that, with his usual insight, he had perceived the origin of my suggestion; perhaps my initiative corresponded in fact to a thought that he had had himself and not dared to put into words; and perhaps he was relieved.

Ordinarily, I loathe these huge places where you have to make your way past the tables, with bored diners staring at you, before you find your friend who, having arrived a few minutes early, will have had the leisure to watch you from his comfortable spot and observe your struggle and your distraught face. I prepared myself for our lunch by introducing a few changes to my usual beauty routine: this time Julien would have the chance to examine me from a distance, a frightening prospect that I had not yet had to confront. I wasn't sure that distance, together with the glare of the ceiling lights, wouldn't make my face look gaunt. I feared that the signs of age and weariness would appear more obvious. I feared that these signs, of which I was very conscious, would prevent contact being made, that we would sit facing each other without connecting . . . What did I not fear? It would be a miracle if, despite so many paralysing anxieties, the meeting was a success. But as often happens, none of what I had foreseen occurred. By some strange phenomenon, the signs that I had dreaded him seeing on my face, I discovered instead on Julien's when, entering the restaurant and alerted no doubt by a sure instinct, I recognised him in the crowd before he had seen me. This piece of luck determined the way the meal unfolded, giving me the upper hand. I made my way confidently towards the table where Julien was waiting, near the door. Alone, leaning back against the banquette where I was to join him, he looked tired, slightly shrunken, as if diminished by the space and the people around him. On seeing me, his face lit up. I sat down beside him, glad that he had had the forethought to choose this seat: our bodies were almost touching, no more was needed for the current that electrified me to pass between us, isolating me from other people, who had now become as unreal, as insignificant as figures painted on a cardboard set. We were alone in the world amongst the crowd, like that evening after our walk in the Bagatelle gardens, when we were still full of the fragrance of roses, in the métro taking us back from Neuilly to Paris – to La Concorde where we parted, still alone together on the packed rush-hour platform. We were careful not to touch, but, nevertheless, impelled by some law of their own, our bodies were constantly meeting, bumping against each other, seeking each other, pushed towards each other. I did my best to exploit the situation by exacerbating Julien's desire. The tension, and the constraint that increased it, made us experience an acceleration of all our faculties that lent a kind of insouciance to our words.

'Your eyes are strange, they seem to be looking into the distance, and you often look a little vague, yet nothing escapes you, you notice the slightest detail, in fact I don't know anyone who sees with such precision, it frightens me sometimes.'

'It comes from my job,' he answered, 'and practice. It's because I've spent so much time looking at the paintings of the great masters. But why should you be afraid?'

And yet, just then, I was no longer afraid of anything, neither his opinion nor his gaze, having recovered a strange state of bliss, like that depicted by Hieronymus Bosch in *The Garden of Earthly Delights*, a painting that I often thought of during the period when I was seeing Julien – an iridescent bubble removed from the world, from time, from thought, from doubt.

He took from his pocket the small pair of glasses with fine gold rims that he had used for some time for reading; like all the things he wore, they had been chosen with care and a sure taste. And to me the little oblongs of glass rimmed with gold, like the soft, dark fabric of the jacket that lay beside him, seemed to denote an innate sense of refinement and elegance, of the same kind as the extreme accuracy of his movements when he touched me, or the slightly curved shape of his little finger that gave his hand a winged appearance, all of these things being expressions of a sensibility that never ceased to move me in the different guises it assumed. The new object became an inherent part of my love. But the thought that I must be mad, since I found in a pair of glasses enough to justify my admiration, did not even occur to me, as love had, at that moment, suppressed in me all critical faculties.

There was only a short time left, once lunch was over, before we had to part. But, so strong was our desire that we felt the need to spend our last few minutes alone together. We hardly spoke during the taxi journey; each instant led us towards the moment we had been waiting for and our attention had room for nothing else. Was the journey long? We drove through streets, squares and avenues as if in a dream, prey to a feeling of unreality which, even more than usual, cut us off from the outside world. At last, closing the door to my flat behind us, we were free to come together. His lips, the softness of his lips, the strength and precision of his embrace, and the work of his hands on my body, caressing, stopping, starting again and sliding, descending, pressing in front, behind, under and between, gently, firmly, insistently. There wasn't an inch of my body, once he'd touched it with his hands or his tongue, that didn't give me a sense of being penetrated. Thus, being beset at all these points, the most sensitive, the most receptive once his hand had awakened them, I was fully open and ready to receive him. We were now half-lying – what succession of movements had placed us thus, I do not know – without taking the time to remove our clothes, my skirt was simply hitched up and I could feel, pressing against the barrier of my underwear, an insistent, imperious thrust. The sequence of movements inevitable. How, when he had just entered me, did he manage to stop, to refuse the climax that both of us were yearning for? I did not help him in this, still occupied as I was with avidly seizing the marks of his love. But then he suddenly stood up; as if to ease my disappointment, or perhaps to increase the sense of deprivation even more, he showed me his bare member, tense and hard. 'Look at the state I'm in, me too,' he said. And with these words we parted quickly, both of us in the grip of the particular tension caused by the frustrating of an instinct. But hardly had we parted than the disappointment came rushing back, a new force filled us (at least this was the feeling that Julien described to me later), an unknown gaiety, lacking during the minutes following the sexual act, carried us through the little incidents of a light-hearted end to the day. Julien loved me, desired me, I had had irrefutable proof of it: nothing else mattered and I was happy. I resolved to resort to such interludes of abstinence every time the need to revive our love was felt. As if he had sensed my calculation without need of explanation, he went along with my suggestions at once, as happy to go for a walk as for us to meet alone in our white room.

31

Affirmation: love as a value

The meetings we arranged during this period of barely
maintained chastity were mostly happy, even if they did
not all achieve the same degree of success. I remember one
beautiful afternoon, towards the end of spring when, seized
by a sudden inspiration, Julien called me at work: he felt
like going to the cinema, to see an old American comedy
– the kind that puts you in a good mood and makes you
feel optimistic, the kind I loved – could I get away from
the office and come with him? I didn't have a second's
hesitation and joyfully sacrificed dull tasks, reasonable
scruples and a conscience that had been dutiful until then,
at the prospect of a few hours in his company – a duty far
more important than any other. A little later, he was waiting for me at the entrance, unconcerned for once about
bumping into people he knew and I, giving myself up to
the euphoria that had come over me on hearing his voice,
went to meet him, freed of all worry, all thought, all feeling other than joy – the joy of seeing him again when the
day had begun like any other and I had not hoped for
anything. This unexpected happiness, combined with the
pleasure of playing truant, rarely experienced as a child,

of snatching from an ordered, predictable life instants of lightness which, for this dual reason, truly partook of the spirit of childhood, I remember it as a special gift, a favour granted us, a brief respite in the midst of the demands of passion – a moment of pure happiness.

It was June, and along the esplanade of Les Invalides the lime trees were in flower. The heat made their fragrance stronger so that, when we arrived there – an area so vast that it made the sky look lighter, more blue – we were enveloped in a sweet-scented cloud, the perfume given off by thousands of lime flowers, as heady and overpowering as that of jasmine on certain summer nights in a village in the South, when old people chat quietly on their doorsteps at dusk and the passer-by pauses to enjoy the murmur combined with the fragrance of the flowers. The scent, like the scent of the roses in the Bagatelle gardens, became associated with that day, increasing its enchantment. In a miraculous way, it seemed to have been given to us as an extra gift. Or perhaps it had been granted us because of the feeling of wonder – the unique wonder of being alive and in love – as if the outside world, recognising our love, took pleasure in celebrating it and moving in unison with it. And our walk, from the Rue de Grenelle, across the esplanade in bloom, then across the Seine, over the Pont Alexandre-III, to the Champs-Elysées, was perfect, glorious, brilliant like the sun that day. Light, we felt light . . . Despite our efforts to walk straight, every step lifted us from the ground, throwing us together, and the winged horses on the bridge and the triple-branched street lamps, the transparent dome of the Grand Palais and the great trunks of the chestnut trees with their tall dark foliage, all these shapes were soaring into the pale sky, stretching, dancing, as jaunty as our pace, while people without solidity or substance passed by, mere extras in our waking dream. Life. To be present in life, intensely. Perhaps its splendour was 'ready beside each person', as Kafka wrote in his *Diary*, but – and I had read these lines with nostalgia – 'veiled, hidden in the depths, invisible, faraway'. I thought that day that love really was the magic that unveiled another world – the world inside the world, the one that is permanently ready by our side, but that we are usually incapable of seeing.

32

The other is my knowledge

During that entire period, I saw Julien little, but hardly felt the anxiety of separation. We were each present to the other; wherever he was, wherever I was, we were always together. The energy of love maintained by our chastity preserved a state of tension within us favourable to love. I had stopped being alone and suffering, absence did not interrupt the sense of a continuous relationship. Julien was in me, not as I saw him sometimes, with his qualities and faults and the traits that charmed me or caused me pain, not with his outward personality, which was continually changing, assuming a thousand different forms, but in his essential being, as my love perceived it, beyond its diverse manifestations. When I was away from Julien, I was able to connect with him again. Then I was no longer occupied with the too-powerful effect of his presence (as one can, after a few hours, begin to appreciate a perfume that was overpowering at first). Starting from the successive fragments that had passed before my eyes that day, I assembled and gradually reconstructed what he really was, winning him back from diversity and change. Having regained, through absence, the man that I loved, I had also recovered his entire presence and the inner unity that the subsequent moments spent with him had taken from me.

I had already marvelled at the fact that love could detect through the appearances and transformations of the personality the more hidden truth, invisible even to the most practised eye, which is like the core of the being and its deepest reality – but it is true that a person can be cut off so totally from that reality that he himself no longer sees it. To the eyes of love, however, it radiated. With Julien I had sometimes been dazzled by the knowledge of it. It was then that I 'saw clearly', not during the hours of resentment when such and such a character trait that I called into question became apparent to me, it was then that I was right.

Thinking about it again from a distance, I realise that I lived this passion on two levels. One corresponded to a form of religion and led me to make great demands of myself, the other followed the bent of my nature which reacted to ordinary incidents in an ordinary way; the jealousy, frustration, possessiveness, pain at absence that constitute the common lot – I experienced them all, of course; despite my repeated efforts to stop myself having these feelings, despite the guilt I felt at experiencing them, they continued to fill me ('As a jealous man, I suffer four times over: because I am jealous, because I blame myself for being so, because I fear that my jealousy will wound the other, because I allow myself to be subject to a banality', as Barthes says).

I see today that such a state of inner division was inevitable; yet I had moments of grace that eclipsed the others by far, when, as if removed from the laws of gravity by the violence of passion, I could feel myself soar and didn't come down from these heights for several days. It was in this state that I chose to show myself to Julien, because this was what love was meant to be and I wanted to be worthy of it. I had therefore strictly suppressed any word, any reproach, any hint that might have let him guess how agitated I was, even if it meant resorting to flight or distance when, unhappy and lost, I had no strength left, so as to regain my composure, to recover the clarity without which I could not live. And Julien was proud of us, proud of the constancy and the depth of feeling he inspired in me, proud of having managed to reconcile a freedom that suited him with a passion which he could not doubt. 'I am loved,' he said to me one day. 'I am sure of being loved.' He would have liked to convince me to share this certainty regarding his feelings for me, he loved me, it was a given, and he assured me that, even if he never saw me again, he would still love me in ten years' time, in twenty years' time – he would always love me. The words 'never' and 'always', though so absolute, did not reassure me, for his serenity, the absence of the anxiety that underlay my love, offered sufficient proof of how different our attachments were and perhaps only total similarity would have calmed me – but then, I would have loved Julien less.

This love, so unequally shared, therefore bore within it

the seeds of failure, if by failure one means the inevitable end. But, as I have said, this was not how I saw it: it mattered to me that I loved Julien, that I loved him so totally that I could not love him more, and that he was fulfilled by that feeling. It mattered to me that I loved, and, in loving, went to the very end of myself, glimpsed a limit, went further still and thus, descending ever further into the deepest layers of my being, gained knowledge that could not be attained by means of the intellect alone. It mattered to me that I had lived to the fullest extent, without sparing myself, without holding back, without being afraid. It mattered to me above all to be able one day to name my need for the absolute.

Love, like suffering, made me progress towards this goal: this is why love was the success of my life, even if none of what I felt was apparent to the eyes of the world and only a tiny part to those of the loved one. That Julien did not have the same sense of revelation in loving made him the poorer of the two: I did not, therefore, envy him the comfort of loving less since the gifts I received were commensurate with what I felt.

Pursuing this line of reasoning a little further, one sees that, having reached a certain level, love feeds on love and no longer depends on its object. I felt a sort of triumph the day I realised that my love was sufficient unto itself. It is true that I sought not only intensity of feelings, but a spiritual path, an outlet to which the sexual act had shown me the way. And then abrupt relapses enlightened me about the value of my elation.

When, passing from this sense of freedom to the image of the man on whom it was based, I wondered about the causes of my passion, I felt surprise and could no longer connect the two: nothing in Julien, whose dimensions seemed suddenly to have been reduced to the point where they were indistinguishable from those of the common run of people, seemed sufficient to justify a feeling that, while based on him, was greater than him, I felt. It all depended on one's point of view. It was against my cold judgment then that I had to battle to restore him to the position where my love had placed him, and I reflected that nuns, in their convent, who never saw God, must have loved with less difficulty. Those of a realistic turn of mind will object that I willingly cultivated the illusion; but I have already suggested how limited the realistic seems to me, and therefore how poor and inadequate. The vision of love is more accurate and more profound in its generosity and commitment to the sublime (as the impulse driving us to give our all is more profound than reason). Disregarding, in a multiple and ever-changing nature, the traits that it finds unpleasant and yet which it sees clearly, it distinguishes those which, worthy of love, remind us, if religion is to be believed, that man was created in the image of God, and thus, isolating in him what is divine, removing him from division and contradiction, it restores the loved one to his original perspective.

Love without end

'*She took my heart, she took me myself, she took the world from me, then she slipped away, leaving me nothing but my desire and my hungry heart.*'

But in fact, Bernart de Ventadour who complains, as was customary with the troubadours, of forever-unrequited love, would certainly not want to be cured of his desire, because love without end, 'the delirium that prevails', is indeed the joy he is so fond of: a desire that never wanes, that nothing can satisfy, that wishes only to embrace the All.

From the point of view of Eros – total Desire, extreme demand for unity – the other, far from being loved in the reality of his distress and hope, becomes an excuse for exaltation, the means of merging with God.

33

Loving and being in love

If I consider how little I saw of Julien at that time, I can only conclude that I had reached the stage where love could do without the presence of the other. I was happy then. The momentum of this happiness awakened my taste for heroism: the will to demand more of myself, in other words to expect nothing of love, to demand nothing of it, to consent to its full freedom.

I sought the company and support that I lacked in my reading of certain mystical texts. Thus I learnt that unhappy love was, in this context, the prototype of all love, since, in its adoring acceptance of its unhappiness itself, it enabled one to attain the 'total disinterestedness of amorous decentring'.

- *Loving someone because he makes me happy*
- *Then loving without paying attention to happiness*
- *Then loving the one who makes me unhappy*
- *The love of God is an unhappy love*

Kierkegaard's *Gradation*, which recounted the stages that I had experienced, did not fail to be enlightening: it provided my blind, clumsy searching and the unhappiness ever ready to be revived with its letters patent of nobility. It also gave me a new impetus which the relative calm that I had achieved would enable me to exploit.

Why in fact had I felt the need to liberate my love, if not because Julien's presence so often proved powerless to appease it? And how many hours of sorrow had I had to endure before I learnt at last to love better, no longer holding back or demanding anything, surrendering all of myself, filled only with the mystical presence of the loved one?

Pure love, the disinterested kind that loves without asking anything in return, that stifles any hope of reciprocity and triumphs over the demands of the self was certainly the ideal that I wished to achieve, the state of purity to which I aspired from then on. Julien had convinced me that really loving someone implied loving him in his freedom, in the states of himself that were beyond your grasp, and not to assuage your own needs (and yet, by requiring that I should respect a freedom that hurt me so much, was he not satisfying his own needs?). Gradually, because Julien made me unhappy, he had prepared me for taking the path of negation of the self, awakening a temptation that had long lain dormant and to which I would soon give myself up entirely. And perhaps such negation seemed like a stage on the way to a detachment which, in itself, appeared desirable – the opposite, more frequent, attitude (namely, rapaciousness, the need to possess) having always horrified me.

That such a love was founded on pain did not surprise me – and it may even have been the pain that gave rise to my desire – for how does one stop loving oneself, how does one achieve separation from oneself, if not by uprooting one's entire being? I was aware of the perversity that such an attitude might imply, but as long as my ideal remained clearly defined, as long as it was constantly in my sights, I hoped not to stop on the way, making suffering my pleasure and my goal. As we shall see, I did not always succeed, and more than once allowed myself to remain stuck in sensations, or be enthralled by discoveries of an entirely different order than that of pure love, since they related to simple psychology.

One day at last, after a meeting during which he had taken even less trouble than usual to hide his abstraction, I was able to write him a letter in which I stated with the utmost sincerity that I had enough love in me to love him in his love for others as well: his wandering desire, never at rest, was an integral part of him, it was linked to the pressure of life within him, to the anxiety for which I had from the very first moment felt attracted to him. It could not be dissociated from him. One day at last, I was able to write him the words that sprang from my pain: 'I have loved you to the point of obliterating my own self – loving the life in you, no longer seeking to be included in it.'

He declared himself 'moved' by my letter, I recall. Such impulses, as I have said, were followed by a return. After my periods of liberty, which was absorption in him, there soon came renewed ardour: Julien wanted to see me again. I was overcome once more by the gentleness of his voice, the certainty of his presence and his power to transform the world. I needed him, humbly needed his moves and his body; far from tearing me from the earth, my love rooted me in it; I was reminded of my fragility and my dependence.

I was thus struck by how precarious my spiritual victories were. Selflessness was an illusion, pure love was an illusion, I thought in moments of despondency, since one always came back to a need that nothing satisfied, not even the presence, not even, I was tempted to add, the love of which Julien assured me. Yet I was aware that these relapses were inevitable, since 'the soul touches but does not hold on to' the great efforts of the spirit. Surely the main thing was never to give up, constantly to re-engage with the truth one had glimpsed?

But at that time I was still far from truly wishing to be cured of a hunger that was the driving force of my life. And, while awaiting the progress I searched as a means of prolonging a demanding passion rather than for spiritual elevation, I was in fact, by these alternating phases, these advances and retreats, these rushes towards pure love and returns of the possessive instinct, increasing the precious, ephemeral tension of desire.

34

Waiting

The time came when the roses in the Jardin de Bagatelle were in full bloom. It was over a year since, on a perfect afternoon, we had strolled through the garden, admiring the flowers without seeing them, like the ridiculous, tender lovers of romantic engravings, both of us very far removed, in those early days, from any ironic self-awareness.

Sitting on a bench, away from passers-by, Julien had gravely assured me that it was possible to love serenely. I had wanted to believe in them, those moments in the rose garden, and in the peace they contained – because with him I was capable of taking on anything and I wanted never to disappoint him; with him, everything seemed possible, even that which by definition was not. Today, measuring the distance travelled, I reflected that, despite my frequent relapses, I had caught glimpses of that serenity, and that if I was by nature unsuited to it, at least I could understand of what it consisted. I still had to face up to a great many discoveries, however, as Julien would apply himself to proving.

A fortnight without seeing him or hearing from him,

interrupted only by a brief telephone call that I made to him in Washington (as usual, he had taken care to give me the names of the hotels where he was staying, with their telephone numbers) in which his voice, distorted by the distance and perhaps by surprise, for he obviously was not expecting my call, gave me the impression that he was in another world, far from my world, far from me, and very busy, required by a new life in which I played no part.

'Let me get my diary,' he said, as he was suggesting we arrange a day and time to meet, and then, cheerfully, I thought: 'I mean, what am I thinking, a pretty woman calls to make a date and I tell her to wait, I need my diary.' The light-hearted tone, so unlike the contemplative mood in which I was making the call, as if, taking me for someone else, he'd given the wrong answer . . . Or perhaps, feeling a million miles from my seriousness, he had playfully slipped into our brief conversation this light note that confused me with the crowd of pretty women, with whom he maintained casual relations, consisting of attacks and sidesteps.

My mistake of course was trying to join him, for this event – a rare one because I so feared wearying him if I called often – for which I had prepared and waited for days (I would be hearing *his* voice), the emotion that this small miracle unfailingly aroused, then the fall that followed, and the dismay (because, hearing him, I had not connected with him again): all of this destroyed (I had taken the risk) my state of happy certainty. Doubt crept in as soon as I compared my love with his, gauging the distance that separated them.

Again I started asking myself questions that were not really questions, since the answers did not in any way alter my dependency. 'Can one go on loving to the point of absurdity according to the law of one's own intensity, without taking into account the loved one's feelings when he, for his part, alternates with ease between forgetfulness and brief returns, loving in a tender fashion that does not in any way hinder the normal course of his life but, like background music that one is aware of without paying it too much attention, serves rather as an agreeable accompaniment to his activities, amorous or otherwise?' Thus, irony in writing sometimes gave me the distance I needed to see the absurdity of an undertaking that consisted in bringing together two people of whom one was devoted to depth, and the other to dispersal, if not escape. But I was no more capable of controlling the forces unleashed than it is possible to stop torrential rain or a volcanic eruption. Appropriately, I recalled my reading of the Romantics, which provided me with satisfying points of comparison and illuminated the turbulence that was convulsing me: in love, as we know, one simply has to let oneself be overpowered, tossed, swept away by the current, sometimes making the most of the whirl to reach, as Julien said one day, 'unknown regions', very far from familiar territory, and this may, moreover, be what holds us and interests us most about the sorrow of love.

During the period that followed his return from the United States, we met fairly regularly. He was sweet and considerate, but I felt he was 'elsewhere'. When I was with him, it was as if there was a pane of glass between us, opaque on his side, transparent on mine, that prevented him from seeing me; these were not the fleeting absences that I had caught in his eyes and had troubled me so, but like a weariness, a heaviness, a slowing of life whose cause escaped me, a fading of the radiance of love; powerless, I witnessed this eclipse of my light. I was too accustomed to Julien's changes of mood and pace to believe that this one, however pronounced, however worrying, would be final, and yet, in the desolate space in which his absence left me, there remained nothing to cling to, neither gentleness nor tenderness. It was then that suffering settled in without giving me respite again. Perhaps it would be more precise to say that I settled into it: because it came from him, it was, for want of joy, an all-powerful link, the incontrovertible sign of his power over me, it was the place where I found him again, where I gauged at every moment the intact power of my love, and I did not turn it away. Dull, heavy, monotonous, this suffering belonged to me and I revelled in it.

Was it not preferable to my former state, my state before I loved him, of stagnation and death? Was it not life nonetheless, as opposed to that void, that death? I feared nothing as much as losing the new forces that had been released within me by love, that they should be exhausted before having borne me towards other discoveries. Maintaining the impetus granted by passion mattered to me as much as loving Julien; the impetus that, tearing me away from habit, had enabled me to *see* once more, and *feel*.

'Had I loved you less, I would simply have fled, refusing the almost permanent pain that is now linked to my obsession with you,' I wrote then, not without dishonesty, for how could I flee? (the letter moreover was not sent). 'Unless,' I added more clear-sightedly, 'I love the pain and I love you through it. Unless it is my true goal and I am using it and you.' I have on occasion, let's be frank, preferred pain to love because of the state of life and clairvoyance that it afforded me. And I reflected that rather than thoughtlessly accusing others of masochism, one would do better to think of the immense benefits derived from one's pain when it is controlled and well understood.

35

To suffer

At that time, probably seeking spiritual succour, I went to
visit one of the people I loved and admired most in all the
world, one of my former professors at university. An old
man now, deprived of the activity that had earned him
honours and prestige – for, in his field, he was one of the
most original minds of his generation – he was therefore
more free with his time when he had once been so careful with it; so the ties that bound us, instead of slacken-
ing, had become tighter. For years, he had watched over
my work and my thinking, seeking less to influence me
than to make me know my own deepest resources. I went
back to him, to his intelligence and rectitude, as to a fixed
point in a shifting, inconsistent landscape, for he had an
ability that I valued above all others and which I felt to
be one of the rarest: the ability to think – not what one
is given to think, but what one discovers alone, face-to-
face with oneself, inspired by one's own experiences,
regardless of the influences blown in on the winds of
change, whether one adopts those influences, uses them
or fights them, far from the prejudices, preconceptions
and other visceral impulses whose justification, through

some specious reasoning, causes such delicious shivers in whoever entertains them in good conscience. I trusted his judgment, knowing that it would never be dictated by envy, the need to protect himself and his own interests, or hidden resentment. And, in twenty years of friendship, I had never been to see him without him giving me, with really astonishing prescience or divination, exactly the support that I needed.

The same went for this visit as with all the previous ones. Had he guessed that I was going through a period of turmoil? I said nothing to him about it (in truth, I never said anything to anyone about it). But, in the conversation, the subject came up, as it was bound to, of love, of suffering and the benefits one could derive from it: sooner or later, one reveals what is occupying one's mind to the exclusion of all else.

'One should be grateful to the people who make us suffer,' he said, and then, with the hint of a question in his voice: 'I hope you're being made to suffer greatly?' A question in which I found neither sadism nor irony, but simply sympathy and curiosity . . . I answered yes, greatly, I must have a gift for it. But suffering, despite what centuries of Christianity would have us believe, is not good in itself; one can undoubtedly make use of it, but also be crushed by it; one can be destroyed by it, I added, thinking of the past few days and my darkest hours.

'It's up to you,' he replied, 'up to you to do something with it once it's been given to you. It depends on you.

There is a vision of oneself that one pays for with one's own pain — a moment of revelation.'

Between two ways of apprehending reality — habit or suffering — I had, whether I liked it or not, chosen the second; and it enabled me to understand and to move forward, whereas before I had felt only the unbearable weight of immobility. I was glad of this progress.

This mood, which was positive when all was said and done, and the relative serenity I drew from it would soon be put severely to the test.

36

Aggression

We still met in the white room to which Julien had taken me the first time, in that slightly elevated, quiet, mysterious district of Paris, pounded like an island by the ceaseless flow of traffic breaking against its small bastions with their closed doors clustering at the foot of the hill, old mansions around which the twentieth century had built its stations and department stores.

I had recently acquired a new flat, a little larger than the previous one, and I was due to move in over the next few days. I wanted to show it to Julien while it was still empty. I imagined his reactions, dreamed of how he would first enter the building with its charming series of small internal courtyards, then mount the staircase made of old varnished wood and, right at the top, go through the front door to the flat, taking possession of those few bare rooms, devoid of atmosphere or influences, as of a virgin sheet of paper where he would write the first sign on which all the others depended. I would merely add a few objects that belonged to me, but the space would always bear the imprint of those first moments when Julien was in it.

But the day he came, I did not, any more than on the

preceding days, feel the current of high tension that usually connected us. What was going on in his life at that time? Was one of the innumerable conjectures in which I had the bad habit of indulging correct? Had he found a new way of satisfying his endless need for love affairs? I never found out. It is likely that he was fully occupied with some new conquest, whose love, perhaps less demanding (but who knows?), made a pleasant change from terrain that had become too familiar and whose rough edges had ended up wearing down his patience. Julien was perfectly capable of conducting several affairs at the same time, giving each in turn the share of attention, then silence required to maintain the tension of love, finding in one something to excite his regret and desire for the other, and in the other renewed strength with which to return to the first. He was always in search of someone new.

The long awaited day arrived. Perhaps I had looked forward to it for too long, desired it too ardently: I seemed to be unable to react. Besides, Julien was in a hurry, abstracted, preoccupied, I thought. Sensing his mood, though my fears might have exaggerated it, deprived me of any possibility of pulling myself together and connecting with him.

We had now entered the empty flat. He was standing at the window, not saying a word. He had punctuated his quick tour of the place with a few trite comments. Within the space of a minute, everything had been seen: there remained only emptiness. Julien was near me, but absent, visibly indifferent, bored perhaps by the situation, sufficiently irritated not to resort to any of the thousand expedients that usually got him out of difficult situations.

I watched him, the minutes passed, each one confining me yet more in my anxiety; nothing happened, nothing arose, no sign, no detail providing me with something to lean on so that I could get back to the outer world. I could see Julien, it was his body, his hands, and the slightly heavy mouth that I loved, his voice and his smile, I could see him, but as someone drowning sees a figure back on the shore, the last vestige of a world to which he no longer belongs, and I felt only loneliness, strangeness and an irreparable distance. The newness of the place, the oddity of the situation – we were facing each other in an unfamiliar empty space – added to this nightmare, that was far more disturbing than the dreams, which were frightening enough, in which I wandered endlessly in search of someone I had lost and for whom haunting regret lingered, rather than their memory. Still today, when I think about it, I feel some of the distress that I experienced then. What hell could be worse than this: to have before one the person one loves most in the whole world and find oneself separated from him by an invisible, insurmountable obstacle? We can dream of someone who is absent, or who is dead, and remember him, but what is left, what hope is there, what recourse, when presence itself is powerless to combat loss? Julien was before me, but I had lost him.

He must have noticed my unease, or perhaps I had

conveyed it to him, for just then he made what later seemed like a hopeless attempt. An attempt, but to what end? Certainly not that of bringing us closer.

Perhaps, like someone who, facing failure, instead of salvaging the situation, does his best to make it worse, Julien felt the need to see this painful experience through to the end, to push it even further and, in a kind of rage, to destroy what we had most loved. Perhaps too he felt a perverse desire to spoil that for which we both had so much respect – the love which we had not failed – or perhaps he simply wanted to get it over with, to change the mood and the pace. These were the explanations that I chose, in preference to another one, even more distressing and much more banal, according to which, mistaking his role and the person he was with, he took me as his partner in one of those simple, efficient little scenes that contemporary novels are so skilled at and that I suspected him of acting out from time to time with pleasure and panache in the company of casual girlfriends. A rapid, brutal scene in which desire, always furious, is supposed to be released. But, in our case, nothing fitted this stereotypical model, and Julien did not seek my collusion.

Mechanically, as one performs a task one is used to, with slightly weary indifference, he made me lie down unceremoniously on the floor and hitched up my clothes. Then he pushed into me.

No ritual directed this violence, neither emotion nor fervour, no desire provoked it, no climax followed; from start to finish, it was sad and unnecessary, and I endured it as one receives a blow — not the blow that brings death of which I had dreamed many times, the high point of life, but its negation. His aggression seemed as empty, as basic and senseless as that of the act of coupling, repeated a thousand times and always the same, when it is deprived of its rituals, and yet, because I compared it to the other times, it seemed also degrading. In the silence that persisted afterwards, we got up without looking at each other, far apart in an alien world. Did he leave feeling he had done his duty?

37

Outlets

The sense of desecration that would haunt me over the following weeks did not come to me then, nor the full awareness of the harm done and endured, but a sort of stupor, of despondency which I would try to fight.

If I am not particularly proud of the solution I chose, neither do I regret it: it corresponded to a challenge, a burst of vitality, an affirmation of the self that had been denied for too long. As I realised afterwards, it was revenge for the many hours when I had voluntarily stepped back. At the time, I felt I wanted to sink even lower and finish destroying what he had begun debasing.

Amongst the men I came across occasionally at that time, there was one whose manner – as if secretly communicating – and conversation – invariably coming back to sex – made me think he would welcome the move I was planning. I hardly knew him, I was not attracted to him, but this indifference suited my resolution. I phoned him on the very day of the scene with Julien. A few hours later, I was knocking at his door. No doubt used to this type of affair, he greeted my suggestion to see him with no surprise. Without wasting time on pointless conversation, he drew me towards the bed, a low divan, I recall, covered in a rough, brightly coloured fabric. This coarse cloth rubbing against my skin is the only sensation that I remember from this meaningless episode. Not that my host proved incompetent; luckily, he was the kind of man who takes the initiative and finds a source of additional excitement in his partner's semi-passive state; an expert in amorous techniques, he played the part assigned to him marvellously well. My pleasure was brief and I was elsewhere. I wanted only one thing: to erase the preceding scene; this was why, in the days and weeks that followed, I had many such encounters, turning to different men – men with whom I had had distant or friendly relations and whom I brought to my new flat, now furnished with the essentials. I met them once, maybe twice, then, realising how pointless our efforts were, I stopped seeing them. From the outset, I announced to each the existence of the others and my indifference. Some were disconcerted, others felt curiosity and a desire to seduce me. I will not describe the day that I went to a district quite a distance from my own where I got lost and wandered endlessly, to the flat of a man whose amorous talents a friend of mine had praised. I had wanted to meet him. He was unhappy at the time, my friend told me, trying to forget a woman who was making him suffer, perhaps our similar situations would create a connection. At my request, she arranged for us to meet.

So I went to his flat. He carried his large, weary body badly; nothing in his appearance or expression suggested

the taste for love that my friend had described in such lyric-
al terms. We sat facing each other, feeling no desire at all,
each as embarrassed as the other, talking without conviction about various things; I noted his look of fatigue, his
mouth, which I found weak and, at the open neck of his
shirt, his loose, grainy skin, and I wondered at the myster-
ies of sex that meant that another woman might take delight
in what I found so unappealing; an overwhelming sadness
was creeping over me, so that it was only with difficulty
that I found the energy to get up and leave.

Of the men I mixed with at this time and, with a new boldness, decided to use, there was one who had shown an
interest in me. He seemed rather shy and awkward, but I
planned to put on a little performance that would give him
the courage to change the nature of our relationship. The
wish to rid myself of my obsession made me imaginative:
I was in need of shock treatment and any man seemed like
a possible recourse. We had arranged to go out for lunch
and I asked him to come to collect me at my flat. It was
summer. I had bought a light, colourful dress for the occasion, low-cut enough to show off my tan but not too
provocative, as he might have found this surprising and
confusing.

I remember his emotion when, after we had been standing and talking to each other for a few minutes, firmly and
full of resolve, he took me in his arms. That day he did
what I was expecting of him; he did so without particular

skill, but with an ardour that comforted me a little, never suspecting that this adventure, won, he thought, by a hard-fought struggle, was part of my plan and that I had carefully prepared it; fleetingly, I thought I had recovered lost momentum, the momentum which love creates, and, more precisely, pleasure, for he too had, though in a less inventive way than Julien, an instinctive skill enabling him to gauge exactly the lightness or weight, speed or insistence, gentleness or force of the caress required at that part of my body at that exact moment. Once again, I was beautiful, alive, enveloped in the radiance given by desire, even in its most basic expression – to be touched, revitalised by desire, was to feel, after arid weeks, the flow of life resuming; and I was simply pleased with this renewed vitality, so different from my great flights of love. And yet, impelled by some perverse demon and following only my urges of the moment, instead of showing him my pleasure as I should, I later behaved very badly towards this man, putting off our meetings at the last minute, according to my whims, slipping hints and half-confidences into the conversation that he must have found perplexing, or withholding without any reason what I had granted him the night before. I don't think I ever sought to take revenge on him for the shifting moods I had endured from Julien, although the thought had occurred to me; I simply did not love him and saw no reason to feign a tenderness that I was too unsatisfied to feel. No doubt he found in me depths of coldness and a good dose of sadism. For the first time,

I was acting without consideration for the other person and I discovered in myself, with a surprise devoid of satisfaction, unknown resources of perversity. Even now, I sometimes feel regret over that ruined relationship and the sorry part I played in it.

My new behaviour, quite unlike the way I usually acted, did, however, restore some of my vigour; it had the principal merit of offering me another image of myself. The banality of my conduct did not escape me: it followed on quite naturally from the unexpected turn our relationship had taken. As for pleasure, it would be wrong to say that I didn't experience any, but I never ceased to be surprised that the sexual act in itself should mean so little when it had, once, assumed such great importance. And the essential current of life that bound me to Julien did not diminish in intensity; on the contrary, it increased with my sadness. What the others gave me made me feel more clearly what they lacked: that which Julien possessed in the highest degree and which was everything. I had never suffered so much.

So this upsurge of rebellion subsided of its own course. I realised how futile were my attempts to escape Julien's power. I had not even succeeded in mitigating the effects of that last scene with him, which had left me with a lingering sense of death and decay. I gave myself up to suffering which engulfed me like a ground swell. A deep, violent suffering such as I had not known before, suffering taken to the extreme, quite unlike ordinary pain or joy.

In fact, it was no longer suffering or even its opposite, happiness, that I sought, but a drug powerful enough to tear me from myself, an instrument of torture sharp enough to cut through the flesh. So that fears and doubts, and defences maintained with great difficulty, and the numerous precautions one takes, should all be destroyed – destroyed the sordid calculations, the need to possess, the jealousy and envy that make the world go round, and all the appalling pettiness in which we are trapped.

I could well understand the mystic nuns of the Middle Ages, who found in destitution, deprivation and the pain they inflicted on their bodies a stimulus, though never cruel enough, to their insatiable hunger for . . . what exactly? For love? For a taste of nothingness, for destruction?

A line that I had recently read in a poem of Rilke's written in French, helped me – as literature, which I did not dissociate from life, always helped me. I repeated it to myself in proportion to how much it soothed me. Each of his words was engraved on my body and I confirmed their truth every minute. Pronouncing them, brooding and mulling over them obsessively, like a machine that looks after itself, eased my sorrow a little:

*Rose qui infiniment possède la perte.**

I possessed loss, to the exclusion of all else and it had indeed opened up an infinity to me. Later, when we had resumed our correspondence, I wrote out for Julien the

*Rose that infinitely possesses loss.

line whose meaning I so fully appreciated. He was delighted with my discovery. 'The line throws me into a state of great elation, admiration and anxiety,' he wrote. 'Where is it from?' He had immediately appropriated it, as the rest of his letter showed, although he had subverted its meaning: he did not dwell on loss, he explained, he did not possess it but, constantly, abandoned it, went beyond it, his nature being made up, precisely, of successive shifts, new developments, abandonments, and it was this abandonment that was visible in him . . . And as he went, he scattered gifts, he gave, he gave to everyone, then he set off again, left, returned, gave again . . . One day he said to me: 'I'm tired of giving of myself in all directions.' As I read his letter, I remembered the exhaustion of which he had complained, and his demanding mission. But I don't think I ever understood how far apart we were, since he had found a way of twisting even this sentence, which contained all of me, to his own advantage, distorting it instead of receiving it.

But what was the use of lingering over definitions of words (loss, for instance, or gift), when a single word, such as love, covers such different experiences? I knew, of course, that one could not 'abandon' loss, as he claimed, at least not if the word loss did indeed cover the experience I was having, but one could perhaps get through it in time by means of a slow and difficult transformation of oneself. And why quibble with him, great consumer of life that he was, with this individual made for flight, constantly in search of new sensations, this celebrant of love, always ready to be filled with wonder, attracted, enthralled and captivated by a new form of life, and then in turn to captivate, and hold? Deep down, I knew full well that it was pointless and that, loving him for the very reasons that made me suffer, I might as well submit – or give up.

To give

*I have wondered about the meaning of the verb 'to give', which
we use so readily and, I find, incorrectly (as we do the verb
'to love'). Holding the attention of others, even by telling
stories that mean a lot to you, takes a great deal of energy;
less, though, than listening to someone else tell stories that
mean nothing to you. 'To give' resembles 'to spill out'. One
spills out what is in one, in other words, one makes a gift of
it (in my reading, I had noticed that psychoanalysts say something similar about the baby on the potty who wants to please
his mother, but I dismissed such inappropriate comparisons).
If one 'spills out' with a specific aim – to please, to seduce,
for instance, to amuse, to captivate – then giving becomes the
equivalent of taking. One 'gives' what one cannot, in any
case, hold back long, with the intention of getting from the
other, first his willingness to listen, his attention, indeed his
admiration, then everything else, his mind in its entirety, like
a ball of wool, a loose end of which one has caught . . . I
have noticed that the people who talk most about how much
they give of themselves are those who demand the most from
us (as it is, they're demanding that we receive what they have
to give, which is no small thing). Who was it who said: 'Is a*

friend not someone who builds around you the greatest possible resonance? Can friendship not be defined as a place of total sonority?'

Friendship, not love. For those words alone, I would admire their author for a long time.

38

Anaesthesia

I was in a state of apathy when I left for my holiday that
summer. Like every year, I headed south, but this time I
went to Yugoslavia, to the island of Korcula.

Dragged away by my usual travelling companions, I left
Paris with indifference; I would have stayed with the same
indifference. For the first time, the beauty of the landscape
left me unmoved. Fringed by tamarisks, the turquoise sea
sparkled beneath a sun that was without nuance or gentleness; empty in the middle of the day, the narrow streets of
the village with their hard white outlines promised a perfection that I could no longer perceive, but whose memory
came back to me, like a signal from a previous life. Only
the evenings brought me a little relief. Below the hotel
where we were staying, a wood stretched down to the sea;
it was there at nightfall that I would go for a walk. All one
could hear, in the growing darkness, was the song of the
cicadas and, with its deep regular rhythm, the breathing of
the sea, ebb and flow, the gentle inhalation dragging the
shingle, then a rumbling that reverberated along the coast.
On quiet evenings I sat under the low branches of the pines
at the edge of the dark, moving water, in magical darkness

pierced here and there by a light, and, endlessly, I listened to the primordial sound of the sea, a rhythm coming from the depths of time, ample and soothing, and its colossal regularity slowly tore me from myself. More than a sense of my own smallness, it was the monotony of the sound that affected me like a powerful anaesthetic, easing my pain and restoring it to its true proportions, mingling it with all the pain in the world of which this eternal movement seemed to contain the beginning and the end. The murmur of the sea on those warm summer evenings, when night after night I went to mingle my grief with it, to wash and dissolve my grief in it, accompanied my reverie from then on, like background music in which the concepts of infinity and indifference prevailed. If this excessively romantic image of a solitary woman (true, I can't write 'young woman', as I would like) thinking of her lost love in a landscape raises a smile, I must say in my defence that those hours of contemplation were utterly devoid of affectation; unhappiness had taken all self-awareness from me: as others do in drugs, I was simply seeking, by any means within my reach, a little respite from my pain.

From time to time, when, having ceased to think about it, I was least expecting it, the suffering returned brutally, and literally pierced my heart. I had the opportunity at that time of confirming the accuracy of the most commonly used expressions in such cases, 'to have a broken heart', 'to be crushed by grief', or 'to have a heavy heart', the heaviness that felt like a weight on my chest, preventing me from breathing . . . But still, thanks to my daily exercises in detachment, I had regained some control of myself by the time I returned to Paris.

So I was soon capable of taking up the threads of my life again with the curiosity that had always prevailed. 'We're not as faithful to the person whom we have most loved as we are to ourselves,' wrote Proust, whose pages on love I read and reread by way of counsel; I still had an intense desire to learn something new, about myself, about life, about others, and it was to that end that I would use my grief. Now being in a position to control it, I wanted, like a miser, to keep it for myself alone: even if I had wanted to I would have been very careful not to write to Julien. The friends that I continued to see regularly must have wondered whether I was not suffering from some secret illness since I looked so unwell, with a permanent air of affliction, but, at that time, I was not tempted to confide in any of them (though, later, discussing him helped me to understand better a character whom passion had loaded with contradictory signs). I took care not to mislay one iota of my grief, not to hinder its progress within me, so that it should open me up to a new understanding. Protected by it, I plunged without stopping into the research I had undertaken. Continuous work acts like a drug; during these days of re-centring, it gave me access to an inner space from which nothing came to remove me. Observed from this centre, people and my dealings with them appeared in a very different light: liberating me from the emotion that they had aroused, distance had restored their true size and place – their truth.

In this state of extreme receptiveness – it was Proust, I think, who remarked that pain raises us from the level on which we normally live – I suddenly discovered the world from a different angle. I now saw in the closed, opaque forms – separate from one another yet vaguely similar – that constituted it, endless possibilities for opening, transition and correspondences: everything echoed everything else, everything was connected, a fast current was circulating, that of the very movement of life. The world was opening up, and had become legible to me. By the action it had had upon me, suffering had become the means of access to an intensified life. Removing the protective layers of habit, it had left my mind 'raw' (as one talks of flesh feeling raw), so that the impressions it received at each moment were inscribed directly upon it. I had never read and understood the poems of Emily Dickinson as well as I did at that time, or the prose of Thomas De Quincey, or any other important book whose music, as that of the sea, brought me soothing and consolation. Every word resonated in me, my understanding of it was no longer external and distant, but deep, intimate, necessary, as if it had been whispered to me by my own experience. I must add that the rhythm of the language, the weight of the words, their order in a sentence, I had the *feeling* that I was discovering all of this; I read these works as if they were being dictated by an inner voice, as if I had written them or was in the process of writing them myself: more precisely, I was living them.

How clearly I saw my story now that I no longer appeared in it, my distress and my silence and my attempts to react as best I could in a situation that I had not assessed. Having given up on my futile struggle, I had no desire to see Julien again, not today, not in a year's time, not in ten years' time . . . He was in me, for ever. It needed no confirmation. That he had not loved me as I had loved him no longer mattered. Any ultimate experience is sufficient unto itself.

This elevated mood prompted other conclusions that I would have liked to hold on to. At the time, they imposed themselves upon me like so many certainties. My new detachment enabled me to discount personal feeling and its effects in order to seize its essence. I firmly believed that the tie that bound me to Julien would escape time as it did its physical anchorage, for it was underpinned by a passion and anguish, by an aspiration that went beyond us both. The very impulse of my love aimed, beyond individual particularities, at the infinite within him: and there I found him again, though no longer seeking him.

39

The letters

Thus, bolstered by this invisible link, I felt shielded from unwelcome emotions. These successive discoveries and the new richness they brought to my life inspired the first few letters I sent to Julien when, after more than a month's silence, he tried to see me again.

First it was a telephone call, one morning when I thought I was safe from that sort of surprise. The phone rang, interrupting me at work, at an hour when it was usually quiet. It was his voice, happy, quick, full of emotion, as if he had only seen me the day before. It was his voice, with its warm, sonorous, well-formed tones, tenderness at times reducing it to a murmur; his voice, but I was not receiving it. It spoke to me of Julien's holidays and of his discoveries, of the Vendée where he was calling from, of his walks to the edge of a land where the horizon receded until it disappeared, tracing a perfect circle around you; he would set out early in the morning, the roads were empty beneath an immense sky, birds were singing, dozens of birds of different kinds, and he felt free. He was vibrant with enthusiasm and the desire to communicate his impressions; he was living, experiencing surprising, unprecedented things ('unprecedented', one of his favourite words: nothing less than extraordinary could happen to him). With its haste, its stops and shifts, with its moments of inspiration punctuated by quiet laughter, his speech evoked a sort of song, a sort of music for me. But after long days when I had taken refuge in the farthest regions of solitude, this song merely seemed like a mockery. Julien had too much sensitivity not to feel that his charm was powerless this time to win me back. And again I admired this Don Juanesque trait: the determination never to let go of a conquest, combined in Julien with a truly astonishing savoir-faire. With rare intuition, he sensed the right moment to step in, and he would not rest until he had once again charmed, recaptured and subdued the fugitive; it seemed to me sometimes that he let her get away only to wield his power all the better; then his divinatory powers prompted him with the words and the tone he needed so that, confused at first, then overcome and reconquered, she soon gave up the fight, and he saw his victim, rebellious a moment earlier, become flustered and return to him. What joy he felt in thus manipulating the women whom he had subjugated, giving them the freedom to escape only to summon them back the next minute – neither too soon nor too late – and he felt grateful to them for providing him with yet more proof of his power. As much as the desire to raise up and console the woman he had enjoyed making suffer, the victory itself moved him. He then showed so much emotion and gentleness that she forgot the last remnants of her resentment: exhausted by so many sudden about-turns, subdued once more, she handed herself over to him and his expertise in matters of love. Here lay the root of Julien's sadism; he never assured me of his feelings with more conviction than when, drained of all strength, I had stopped hearing him. And it's true that he loved me best at such times: through cruelty he had succeeded in arousing his desire. And, throwing off all fetters, I opened myself up entirely to the explosion of joy. I knew then that the long weeks of distress that I had lived through had existed only to result in those hours when I went back to him.

Time in our meetings was not the same as everyday time and the reality in which I joined him had no more to do with usual experience than a moment of heightened perception has with ordinary life. I was therefore ready to suffer if suffering was the price of those hours of release. And who can say of a woman who consents so willingly to the game on which her life depends, that she is a victim? I saw myself more as a partner in a drawn match, if not as the permanent winner since, in effect, I gained so much more from the game than Julien, whose moments of illu-mination, because he loved less, were no more than a distant reflection of my own. Besides, I have always thought that those who, from fear of suffering or being duped, refuse to give themselves up to the game and try constantly to control it, are the ones who are the dupes in the end: the share of life, love and death that is allotted to them is so much narrower than for the others, those who live and feel in proportion to how much they have risked.

Doubtless we can see here the reasons for the duration of a passion that, so often, threatened to come to an end. Whatever I may have thought of Julien, whatever my reproaches and the negative aspects of the relationship, none of it managed to jeopardise the moments of love. No link exists between feelings inscribed as the days pass, whose motives can easily be analysed, and the impulse coming from unknown regions that lifted me when I saw him. Similarly, it was not the sum of his qualities and faults, as I've said, that I loved in him, but his being, which was something else that I perceived in moments of pure presence.

This time though the magic wasn't working, I felt nothing, despite my efforts my voice remained flat and distant. So he brought his descriptions to an end and, making a last attempt to reach me, carried along also by his momentum, he used an infallible means – assuring me of his love:

'I love you very deeply,' I heard him say, 'and I have been dying to tell you. Even if I never see you again, it would do nothing to change the fact that I love you very deeply and always will.'

I did not doubt his sincerity for a second. In his unreliable and dangerous way, Julien loved me and, for as long as I had the strength and the desire to continue, to suffer and to let myself be recaptured, he would never leave me. I understood then what he expected of me. One day, before love crumbled under the effect of time and lassi-tude, before it turned into a tolerant sympathetic friend-ship, loaded with confidences that I did not want, I would have to leave again so as to preserve its integrity.

A few days later, I received a letter. Its pages ended with an 'objective comment', 'I want you so much', which, despite the neutrality of my responses on the telephone, marked a progression and, even, an offensive. The image of a man alone, setting out for the marshes to watch the birds, completed the cheerful missive, which made me dream, desire, hope (he had always had the knack of constructing these little scenes that served his image admirably and showed him in all his uniqueness, gripped by some powerful emotion, full of life, filled with wonder or overwhelmed by fate). But he had to make a greater effort to reach me, for, this time, I had travelled so far alone for so long that I was no longer capable of follow-ing him in his twists and turns. It was the beginning of a long correspondence. In it I indulged in a sublime tone, while remaining utterly sincere. Julien had asked me to explain. I insisted that I was neither his victim nor his play-thing, and that I was free in the face of my suffering – free to do with it as I thought fit. It was his gift to me. It was up to me to utilise it to the best of my ability, to adapt it for my use.

I remember my second letter in particular; there was not a single word in it that I had not pondered at length, not one word that did not express, from the depths of my heart, an imperious need for inner clarity. When I had written it, the air seemed lighter and I felt that I could breathe more freely. Still today, I can easily reconstruct the main part of the letter.

'Please never say, never think, that you have harmed me. That would be so far from the truth. It didn't depend on you to do me harm. To make me suffer no doubt, but it was up to me to transform that suffering; and I have done so. And anyway the suffering was *in harmony* with everything else, with the surges of joy, as deep, as full, and going beyond any precise cause: a sort of airing of the spirit after years that were constricted, years of shallow breathing. No, it has not "harmed me", as it has been an intensification of life, a means of access to a stronger vision. Only boredom and the absence of love are unacceptable. Also, when you think of me, please don't tell yourself that 'from now on, you want to do me only good', as you wrote, but that you have already done me *all* the good that you could by making me love you with such intensity, and therefore, unavoidably, making me suffer . . .'

This letter, which absolved him of all guilt, must have pleased Julien: he thought it 'immense' and kept it with him for a long time.

This time, he wanted to submit entirely to my will and leave it to me to decide when we would meet again. I didn't think about it long. The hours of struggle of which I had recently been so proud now seemed hard and desolate, utterly inadequate compared with the gentleness filling me once more.

40

Alternation

On the train from Paris to La Rochelle, I thought of nothing but him. I was divided between the agitation into which I was thrown at the thought of seeing him again, and the fear – no less great – that my initiative would come up against unforeseen difficulties. When I made the decision to go to him, I had not thought it necessary to warn him, relying on him being happily surprised, when I called him, to discover that I was suddenly so near. But as the train drew nearer, my anxiety increased and formed precise questions: would he find a way to interrupt the unvarying rhythm of days by the sea with his family, between the beach, walks, reading and meals, and get away to see me, even if only for an hour, a few minutes? And would the break in his peaceful, ordered life not cause him more nuisance than pleasure, even if every one of his letters proclaimed his desire to share the land-scapes and the light he loved with me?

Once in the small hotel room where I had found refuge, such was the conflict between my feelings and my need for Julien, that I was hesitant to go to the telephone: my heart was pounding in my throat, my voice would be unrecognisable, he would not be alone or, worse still, he would be out and somebody else would answer . . . So much so that I almost left. And yet, more dead than alive, a million miles from the happiness that I had imagined, in the end I picked up the menacing instrument and dialled his number. By chance, it was Julien who answered. I heard his voice – his calm, happy voice, not in the least surprised: 'My darling', surrounded by the light breath that gave the words, whenever he pronounced them, the force of a declaration, 'How lovely to hear your voice, I was just thinking how much I felt like talking to you . . .' I then heard myself say the words I had prepared: 'I'm here, a few streets away, I've just arrived . . .'

Something was happening at the other end of the line, an upheaval that was only conveyed by an inarticulate exclamation followed by a silence of several seconds after which a strained, quick, insistent voice went on: 'Come. Straight away. No, wait a minute . . . Let me think . . .' We had to avoid bumping into anyone, wait for the right moment, when his family would be busy with their usual evening activities. We agreed to meet at dusk, on the outskirts of the village, at the fence where the marshes began . . .

When I hung up, I felt dazed. I stood in the middle of the bare hotel room, giddy with happiness. A few weeks earlier, I had thought my life over and had taken refuge in haughty solitude: all that I had left was the prospect – not too pleasant, admittedly – of inner progress patiently achieved. A few minutes earlier, I had felt oppressed by the fear of displeasing him, had been prepared to return to Paris as rapidly as possible. But now everything had changed: within the space of a second, simply by the grace of love, I had gone from prostration to euphoria. Life was opening up, it was fresh and blue like a sunny early morning, rich in possibilities that all came down to this one incredible event: seeing him again. I was going to see Julien again, there was no other reality.

Thus my mood swung vertiginously, love transporting me as if by magic from one state to its opposite. After the dark days when I thought I had lost Julien, space expanded, walls disappeared, I felt nothing but joy. Concentrated in a single moment, it was more happiness than I could bear. I regretted only that its surge deprived me of the awareness I needed to assess the extent of the change; but over the following weeks I would return tirelessly to these emotions and these scenes, breaking them down and pondering them, playing and replaying them in my memory, stopping at each image, reflecting on each word so as to savour it, dwelling on such and such a tender intonation and the pleasure it had afforded me.

I left the room because I was suffocating. My happiness needed to pour out in the open air. I wasn't walking, I was flying, dancing. More than ever, the external world seemed like a backdrop, unreal. While waiting for the evening, in order to work off some of my excitement, I wandered through the streets, the squares of the village, the interlacing of alleys lined with low, white houses. The sky – light, blue, huge above the flat roofs – gave anyone walking beneath it the feeling of being lifted, enveloped, drawn up into its heights, as if partaking oneself of the nature of the air.

Every step brought me nearer to Julien; he had taken these routes that I was following, he had looked at and loved this corner and that house, he had stopped before this dead end, and had then walked on, perhaps, ready to discover some masterpiece, some abandoned garden half-hidden behind a long wall. I felt that he had taken care to put this decor in place, anticipating the moment when I would come to join him there. He was its creator, he had intended it for me and was now giving it to me as a gift: in every thing it was his presence that I sensed, in every thing it was Julien that I loved. My walk had no aim save this reunion, preparing me for the moment when I would see him again.

At nine o'clock, as the sun was setting and the last passers-by were heading home, I went, as if in a dream, to the place where we had agreed to meet. A cool wind was blowing and along the road the tall grass in the fields bent over. And the outlines of the landscape stretching as far as the eye could see, the wind and the light, and the few people hurrying past, were nothing but a projection of my strange state. At last I saw a slim figure in the distance, leaning on the fence – Julien waiting for me.

We walked side by side along the narrow path, between the flat expanses of salt marsh. We stared straight ahead at the line where land, sky and water met. On the horizon, like fine black piping, land separated the vault of the sky from its reflection in the pale water. It described a vast circle around us, just as Julien had said, and we were, like the point of a compass, at the centre of this world. From time to time, turning towards him, I saw his profile lit by the light of the waning day: both near and far away, thus outlined against the dark blue sky, he seemed to assume a new nobility, to have something of the peaceful eternity of these borderlands. Everything was at rest, absolutely still. Gradually the stillness spread to us, soothing the mood of euphoria that a little earlier had taken us out of ourselves. Night was falling now, shrouding the slow stealthy life that exuded a powerful odour. We were alone. Far from the human element, we had entered a new realm, a watery universe pierced now and then by the wild calls of birds. Motionless and perfect, the hieratic form of a great grey heron appeared to be waiting. Sometimes, the cry of a gull taking flight emphasised the profound loneliness of the place. Just below the level of the road, immense rectangles in which the sea was retained offered up their curiously varied surface. The sky was reflected in them and from all sides, the eye, as far as it could see, found nothing but this gentle flatness. A long-drained marsh evoked a piece of African land transported there by the greatest chance, with deep cracks separating little islands of grey silt at regular intervals.

Julien stopped suddenly and, taking hold of my arm, pointed out the iridescent colour of the mud, where the water was less deep: reddish-brown or greenish foam indicated the decaying of leaves, strata of vegetation slowly rotting, forming a thick, moving paste, but life was emerging from this heavy matter, mixed with the fermentation of decay, rising in outcrops of indefinable hues. Clusters of bubbles, sinuous trails, twisted patterns spreading over the surface of the green water. Peering at these patches of algae and mud, one had a sense, Julien remarked, having observed them closely, of returning to the origins of the world, of finding oneself before the natural laboratory from which life had slowly emerged.

In the verges, beneath the tamarisks, there grew a carpet of grasses and marsh samphire. It was here that we hid, behind tall bushes that formed like a rampart in places, between the dry earth path and the dampness of the mud.

For the first time we were not in an enclosed space with walls protecting our secret, but in the open air, exposed, out in the elements, merging with them, with the powerful smell of sea, with the darkening horizon whose distant line was melting into the night, with the liquid immensity surrounding us, with all the teeming, silent space.

Julien embraced me, clasping me violently. I kissed him in the mouth for a long time. We clung to each other. I don't know what it was that made us stagger – the wind that had risen, the boundless sky, the force of our embrace or the earth shifting and sliding beneath our feet. As I fell, I could feel beneath the layer of grass the spongy ground receiving me. Julien stripped me to my stomach and the cold night air settled upon me; then I opened myself up and he pushed into my body brutally, massively, in a single, sure, heavy movement that pinned me to the ground. He was giving me the life that I had been waiting for, and the night and the smell of mud and the wind blowing across the expanse of marshland, the cries of a last few birds and the shiver of the darkness, he was giving me the starless, limitless sky, and the earth whose damp pressure I could feel against my back, he was giving me all the pulsing of the universe in us, around us.

Julien was catching his breath, pressing down on me without moving. Suddenly, he gripped me more tightly. With unprecedented violence, he bore down with all his weight; as if to finish me off; one last time; the final explosion beyond which nothing remained; I heard myself cry out.

He got up with difficulty. I clung to him, my limbs heavy; I was now kneeling, my face on a level with his bare stomach; I explored its firmness and its softness with my lips, kissing it, probing it lightly over its entire surface; below, I kissed too that which always caused a rush of emotion, his sex, erect once more. My knees planted in the ground, my arms clasped around his loins like a supplicant.

Then I drew Julien to me and again we rolled to the ground. The damp earth stuck to our bodies and this excited us no less than the nakedness of our flesh, its lunar whiteness contrasting with the black grass.

At last, we lay beside each other, without thought, without desire or memory, at peace.

41

Escape

On the train back to Paris, reliving these surprising scenes, I could not help thinking that they marked the peak and decline of a feeling.

So, while the memory of the last few hours we had spent together still sustained me, I made the decision on that return journey to leave Julien – not because sorrow was forcing me to do so, but because happiness was giving me the courage: the courage not to fail love. And would it not be failing to accept the sterile, futile, appalling suffering I had glimpsed, suffering which might end up distancing me from him and, this time, losing him and losing myself as well? Would I not do better to go deeper into myself so as to extract the full meaning of the most important love affair I had ever had and to continue loving him in the love he had revealed to me? And to withdraw, with the memory intact of our most intense hours on which my mind could then focus?

How different those hours (so full, dense, dreamy that nothing, neither happiness nor unhappiness could slip into them) were from the days of coldness when I thought I didn't love him any more – days when, unable to detach my thoughts from him, I suffered alienation and power-lessness: I could not break out from the all-too-familiar circuits that I had travelled to the point of nausea, and which all led back to the same question: how much does he love me? The humiliation of a mind in the grip of a single obsession, condemned to returning to the same tormenting question that it would give anything to escape – as I saw it, this was my punishment for a possessiveness that I could not avoid.

I felt enriched by a victory that *nothing would ever be able to take away from me* and which, in my eyes, merged with life itself. Was it not life, with its dual secret, both physical and spiritual, that Julien had given me? And was not each stage that he had me discover, even absence and return, like a stage in an initiation into the amorous life and the knowledge that follows? During the course of an education that was both exhilarating and painful, he had revealed to me the sacred nature of love and desire and the incalculable power concealed within them – the power to change the world and to bring back to life that which was dead.

I recalled what he said to me one day with a solemn look: he had made certain women he had loved gain access to regions of themselves whose existence they did not even suspect. This indeed was his vocation: to awaken the chosen one to awareness, to bestow his knowledge upon her. I understood the silence in which he had surrounded love, and the ritual that he engaged in, and the violence of an activity whose portent had so surprised me: it was one more proof of his skill at sex and his ability to control it. For if the only motive of the violence had been a need to attack and its only aim the liberation of that instinct, it would not have possessed to that degree the precision that situated its effects so exactly between pleasure and pain. It would not have been followed by displays of tenderness that lessened, even reversed the sense of an assault. But Julien kept us to the dangerous dividing line between an attraction to darkness (to which one night I had, however, had such a great desire to yield) and the resistance still offered to it by consciousness — a resistance without which, regressing to a primitive state, we would have acted with degrading brutality.

The power to rouse hidden forces by means of a movement (a blow, an attack, a provocation), the always difficult control of an equilibrium — these were the qualities for which I compared Julien to a high priest, a master of ceremonies, possessing also their gravitas, their shadow of sadness and their detachment. Had he skirted danger less closely, we would not have experienced the feeling of terror; and had he not himself yielded to the impetus, the ritual would have remained futile — empty and external. If he had let himself be controlled by these forces and had for a moment ceased to exercise vigilance, then, far from the ceremony in which every movement is taken beyond itself by the meaning it assumes, we would have sunk into an endless, exhausting quest for pleasure.

Just as, aware of the risk of our getting stuck, of losing ourselves in such a quest, he had guided me beyond it with a sure hand, I had tried, instructed by his science and in turn taking the initiative – by seeking out situations where desire had to be curbed, suppressed – to increase, to recharge it. And, without need of explanation, he had fallen in with my proposal from the outset, entered into the spirit of my little game, taking it even further than I had imagined.

In my view, the scene that took place in the marshes assumed a particular meaning. We had not sought to make the event seem new through the strangeness of the location where it took place – that outermost edge of land already penetrated by the sea, that last outpost surrounded by the ocean. It was there nonetheless, protected by the night, that I experienced most intensely one of the singular powers of love: the power of opening us up to the world, of merging us with it. This is what I had once felt, doubtlessly in a different way, during my solitary summers in the woods as a child.

42

To renounce

I sensed nothing religious in Julien in the narrow meaning of the word, but did not his gift for being intensely
alive at every minute of existence, his power to reinvent
himself continually beyond sadness and anxiety, and
which therefore implied both, correspond to a sort of religion of life, a way of serving it? Love, as he conceived
of it, was the means of access to true life, a way of celebrating it, an act of giving thanks. A certain amount of
heroism was implicit in his fervent resolve to conquer it
and give himself up to it: he fought to preserve the 'state
of love' within himself and to bring to others, as he put
it, 'a little light' – the light that came to him from such
a state. This was why I had recognised Julien as the celebrant of a very ancient cult, entrusted with an essential
secret whose nature he had fully assessed. The tortured
tenderness that I sometimes saw in his face, I linked to
the difficulty of his undertaking or, more precisely, to the
demands of his vocation.

And it is true that in moments of euphoria, when I was
free of my tormenting need for him, I thought the main
thing was that he loved me, that we were linked, never

separated and that, through him, I could be part of the amorous life, the life-in-a-state-of-love that he was so skilled at creating and maintaining. The greater the pleasure, the less self-interested the love it produces. As long as I was granted that light, what did it matter if others too received it from him, I told myself in a surge of gratitude, and was not the important thing that, escaping the stagnation, the inertia, the death-in-life endured for so many years, I should dwell in the lightness that he had so generously had me enjoy – that I should remain *in life*?

Sometimes, seeing him exhausted by what he discreetly referred to as 'my funny old life', which was in fact the multiplying of his love affairs, with the duty of giving each woman what she expected, I had stood by him, 'fraternally', as he had requested. Had he not asked me to help him, begging me to feel compassion for him, if need be letting out a moan at a recent blessing that was also a burden? I felt then that we were like two priests serving the same god. And yet, my identifying with him did not last long: if I loved love, I loved the man it depended on even more; soon the goal was obscured since I lacked the means of attaining it – the simple human love of which I lacked proof, or at least proof in which I could believe, in other words Julien's exclusive love for me.

I had glimpsed the paradoxical truth that to preserve in myself the amorous life, I would first have to renounce it. I had written to him one day that the need to surpass myself was the very form of my love for him. And now I would, beyond my specific attachments, have to try to move forward in the direction that they had revealed to me.

43

Obliteration

The only glory of which I could boast (it was one, at least in my eyes) was that I never fell into the banality of reproach, complaint, endless futile arguing, rancour and hatred. In fact, I wanted him to go on loving me, as he had promised, and I didn't want his love to be weighed down, ruined by the scenes at the end (that wish was granted: for years, a word, a sign of life and tenderness sent by Julien from time to time provided the proof). My only revenge – I had long pondered it, for I wanted Julien to miss me – was wishing to leave him an intact and never fully decipherable image of me. Quite a few weeks after my departure, he wrote as if it were a revelation to him: 'Really, you've never stopped suffering'; it wasn't true, of course, but, for a moment, I was delighted, because his belated curiosity proved that I had managed to preserve love's secret.

Indeed, it is easier to leave in mid-triumph than to accept a separation when it is imposed upon you. Yet I was incapable of leaving at the point when I made the decision to do so.

Not that Julien ever expressed a wish that I should leave

– I think he would even have tried to stop me – and in a sense, I left only when forced to because of exhaustion, when I had no more strength, in a final burst of the vital instinct which I had, however, so often lacked, weeks and months, two years, in fact, after I had made my decision, in the elation of a day of success when we had loved each other completely. My vague attempts to leave always ended in a return: we need only carry out this intention for the strength we believed we had to disappear and the vitality of a love that had seemed moribund to become apparent. I had no sooner resolved to leave Julien than the impossibility of doing so was revealed to me together with the depth of a link entwining, I felt, the very roots of my being.

What I had asked of love – to be freed from myself – I had achieved: I was effectively absent but empty, relieved of thought, unburdened of memory, and what remained of the feeling of grace that had carried me beyond days, what remained of the love that had filled and occupied me? Indeed, what remained of it when all I could see was the limitless, arid extent of a love without love of which nothing could free me? I had unfailingly followed the rules laid down at the start, rules inspired by our common need for an intensity that was in fact a striving for the Absolute. Had the striving fully occupied Julien, my love would have found nothing to practise on and, on the other hand, it would have lost heart had Julien not, like me, constantly set off again after failing. And we did, sometimes, succeed in our effort.

And now, this exhaustion: obliteration, a complete blank. Like crossing the desert. I could not see what new sound to produce, what fresh new thought, what unknown hope to entertain other than that of oblivion, even though this was something I did not want. Love, having become an obsession, no longer allowed me to see, beyond the person of Julien, once the intermediary of the sacred. I had stopped perceiving life because I was filled with nothing but distress at this man's absence.

Could I accept such an ending to an affair, which, while doubtless banal in itself, had, in the way it had provided me with insights, assumed a high significance, a high degree of reality? In order to escape a sterility that was at variance with the very calling of this passion, I owed it to myself to push my search further, away from the to-and-fro which, once it had played its part, had made me suffer: I owed it to myself to find the path of love again.

44

Alone

To speed up the effects of time, bringing detachment, though too slowly, and to give me a chance of escaping the signs of gratitude that Julien sent me regularly and that I still found troubling, I resolved to leave Paris.

He had continued to write to me. His letters gradually became confiding, though without revealing the new affair that was requiring all of him: excited by the onset of a new feeling and already turned towards a different future, he still laid claim to me from a distance, unable to resign himself to letting me go, eager to convey his discovery without spelling it out, to link me, even if only through my jealousy, to what he was experiencing. One letter told me of the truly 'atrocious' dilemma that he was in, since he could neither talk to me nor keep silent. He was suffering death and passion and – evoking, always in veiled terms, both his love for another woman and the love he still felt for me – he portrayed himself as a victim in the grip of confusion in which, I knew, however, he found renewed energy.

Like the conductor of an orchestra, he had to control every note: the fading or, even worse, the silence of one of the instruments at his disposal would have conclusively compromised the harmony of the complex whole that was his life. He therefore took care to maintain my attachment to him so that this major link should not slacken. And then, even though he was in love with another woman, he had to share with me feelings in which I played a part, strengthening his love for me in his nascent love for her, just as he intensified his new passion with all the confusion into which he was thrown by the need both to hide things from me and to have me picture them.

And yet I chose this time to stop responding to his need for me, not that his need had stopped affecting me, but for a long time now Julien's demands had prevented me from remaining faithful to the spirit of love as he had revealed it to me – a spirit based not on wrenching pain, but on joy, fulfilment.

So, having sold the flat associated with memories of him, I left. I left without setting a date for my return. After years of service, the official body for which I worked had agreed to give me a year's leave. Some savings, that I would supplement by means of an article published from time to time in a newspaper, would enable me to provide for my needs, which were modest anyway. A friend had lent me her house in a village in the south of Italy. I decided to move there for the next few weeks or months.

I don't know whether it was the beauty of the country, the sudden change of scenery or the light that located the landscape out of time, dispelling sadness and ghosts, but as soon as I arrived I felt better. Having left Paris in the cold and grey of February, I greeted the sudden flood of light after months of darkness and confinement as a kind of miracle. The air was gentle, I breathed it in. Every detail – the glinting of the sun on the sea in the morning, the bright fruit amongst the dark foliage of the orange trees, the sweet, fresh smell of the first freesias – evoked a pleasure that was combined with the pleasure of being alive. Nothing mattered any more, only my awareness of the flower's scent or the tree weighed down with oranges . . . As I knew no one, I could live in the seclusion that I wished for. I spoke only to order a meal from time to time or buy a few provisions, took long walks by the sea and gradually let the silence settle in me.

Always present, Julien's image no longer obscured the landscape, no longer came between me and the world. Far from having its contours erased by separation, his image accompanied me at every moment of the day and, now that the bleak suffering of the last few months was easing, I could return at length to each expression, each gesture that was so familiar to me. I pictured his anxious look, the expectation in his eyes, and the way he had of settling himself to listen to me, ready to laugh and be amused by the anecdotes that I had collected for the moment when I would recount them to him, and a thousand other details and attitudes whose memory I summoned freely and which, every one, restored to me in all his unity the person that I loved. This unity, I had it back at last, just as it had come to me once in the simple inflection of his voice on the tele-phone, his voice that reached me like a certainty compared to which nothing else counted.

Disregarding the hours of jealousy, the fits of grief and bitterness, and the heaviness of blind weeks, my memory retained only the loftiest aspect of our love: the joy he had brought me. It fully restored to me the grace of loving.

But instead of love being limited to a single person who eclipsed the rest of the world, condemning this world to being no more than a backdrop, the amorous state, in my new freedom, was transmitted to beings and things, to all that I saw. It coloured my reactions and my outlook, as if a magic filter had been placed over my inner eye: I felt an effusive love for everything that existed.

It was undoubtedly a specific person that I loved, but my love, which could do without the body of the other and the support of his presence, the swings between joy and disappointment, radiated well beyond its source, infus-ing everything around me with another reality. Because it was purified of all that was not it, of all that, embodying it, weighed it down, subjecting it to contradictory needs and, therefore, to pain, my liberated love now lit up every-thing. Thus transformed, it circulated so freely that at every moment, as in the poetic vision, it revealed to me the beauty of the object viewed – usually veiled by habit and distrac-tions – and the novelty of every episode of the day, and the incredible profusion of the world around me.

In particular, I remember the strange change in the

pleasure of taste, a pleasure to which I had so far paid little attention. If I tasted a piece of fruit, it melted on my tongue 'like a thought of the mind that dissolves', since the sensation overcame all of me, affecting my mind as much as my body. If I inhaled the scent of a flower, it spread through all of me, 'going to my head' as is so aptly said. Absorbing the fruit, smelling the flower were like being penetrated by life via the senses of taste and smell – a form of communion with the land that I loved. This penetration, affecting the senses, was also of a spiritual nature, it included the entire person. And, in this, it echoed the sexual act which so perfectly realises that which our mind yearns for: to be penetrated – body and soul – by the one we love. And this need to be filled with life, as one fills a cup to the brim, how strange and, as it were, simple, even crude, that the physical configuration of the woman should represent it so exactly – by a void, a hole, an absence that is a call. It was truly astounding that the body should enable us so precisely to satisfy this need: that the hollow at our centre could be filled physically, spiritually, pleasure rising to the same level in the visible and invisible channels.

Such thoughts applied to the simple actions of eating, breathing, seeing, made them like a reflection and prolongation of the act of love and, through love, they gave unity to that which otherwise existed only in fragmented, divided form. And thus, instead of declining because it was deprived of its source, my love for Julien grew all the time in contemplation.

Continence, which I had once sought in order to increase desire, did not weigh on me in the slightest now that it was imposed. Our relationship with the landscape is erotic, I had noticed it before: trees and flowers awakened in me a little of the joyous vitality, of the happy desire that was once focused on the person of Julien. I lived, therefore, in a state of love. As with poetry, this state restored radiance to the world such as I had occasionally glimpsed but which now never dulled.

I suddenly felt an urge to write to Julien to tell him of my surprising discovery – the revelation of an amorous state that, like everything else, came from him. In order to be entirely honest in this letter, I would have had to add that my love could do without him, and even required that I never see him again. But then, why write to him? Julien was in me for ever, this was the reality I had decided to confine myself to, the reality that had enabled me to recover a little peace and overcome my feeling of death. Undoubtedly I knew that the state of grace I had now regained was also ephemeral and that I would have to strive constantly to recapture it, ever relapsing and beginning again. But I did not discount the thought of moving towards a spiritual search, something that had always attracted me, love now specifying its form and meaning.

Because I knew that Julien would understand, I decided never to write to him again, never to see him again. I knew that he, better than anyone, would understand the joy that love brought me, not the joy that requires a presence and

Covert Investigation

Centre for Applied Sciences Library
City & Islington College
311-321 Goswell Road
London   EC1V 7DD

CITY AND ISLINGTON
COLLEGE

Email: scilib@candi.ac.uk
Web: www.candi.ac.uk

This book is due for retum on the date last stamped below.
You may renew in person or by email. Please quote your Student ID
number and the book barcode number. The book may not be
renewed if required by another reader.

Fine: 10p per day

WITHDRAWN

CPD6017